APOCALYPSE

THE PHOENIX EDITION OF D. H. LAWRENCE

Novels:

THE WHITE PEACOCK
SONS AND LOVERS
THE TRESPASSER
WOMEN IN LOVE
THE RAINBOW

AARON'S ROD
THE LOST GIRL
KANGAROO
THE PLUMED SERPENT
LADY CHATTERLEY'S LOVER

Short Novels:

Two volumes containing:

LOVE AMONG THE HAYSTACKS
THE LADYBIRD
THE FOX
THE CAPTAIN'S DOLL

ST. MAWR
THE VIRGIN AND THE GIPSY
THE MAN WHO DIED

Travel:

Three volumes containing:
TWILIGHT IN ITALY
SEA AND SARDINIA
MORNINGS IN MEXICO and ETRUSCAN PLACES

Short Stories:
In three volumes

Essays:

Three volumes containing:
FANTASIA OF THE UNCONSCIOUS and
PSYCHOANALYSIS AND THE UNCONSCIOUS
STUDIES IN CLASSIC AMERICAN LITERATURE
APOCALYPSE

THE FIRST LADY CHATTERLEY
JOHN THOMAS AND LADY JANE
(*the first two versions of Lady Chatterley's Lover*)
PHOENIX: THE POSTHUMOUS PAPERS OF D. H. LAWRENCE
(*edited by Edward D. McDonald*)
THE LETTERS OF D. H. LAWRENCE (*edited by Aldous Huxley*)
SELECTED LITERARY CRITICISM (*edited by Anthony Beal*)
THE COLLECTED LETTERS OF D. H. LAWRENCE
(*two volumes, edited by Harry T. Moore*)
THE COMPLETE POEMS OF D. H. LAWRENCE
(*two volumes, edited by Vivian de Sola Pinto and
Warren Roberts*)
THE COMPLETE PLAYS OF D. H. LAWRENCE
PHOENIX II: UNCOLLECTED, UNPUBLISHED AND OTHER PROSE WORKS
BY D. H. LAWRENCE
(*edited by Warren Roberts and Harry T. Moore*)

D. H. LAWRENCE

Apocalypse

WITH AN INTRODUCTION BY
RICHARD ALDINGTON

HEINEMANN : LONDON

William Heinemann Ltd
15 Queen Street, Mayfair, London W1X 8BE

LONDON   MELBOURNE   TORONTO
JOHANNESBURG   AUCKLAND

Printed in Great Britain by
Northumberland Press Limited, Gateshead

INTRODUCTION

To Frieda Lawrence

Dear Frieda,

I've undertaken to say something about *Apocalypse* and about Lawrence, and I've decided that the best way to do it is by a letter to you. There are two clear advantages. If I say anything which you know to be false or malicious, you are thus invited to come out and say so publicly. And by making this Introduction an informal letter, I can at least try to avoid that quasi-professorial solemnity of the intellectuals which annoyed Lawrence and which is so unsuitable when writing about a free spirit who loved life.

Such a lot of nonsense has been written about Lawrence, as well as stuff which is either stupidly uncomprehending or downright malevolent. I don't want to add to any of it. Yesterday I was reading a new life of Edgar Poe, where the man shows that most of the discreditable stories about Poe are either unproved or demonstrably untrue; and that the worst fabricator was his own literary executor! This made me think of the ridiculously false and cruel things which have been written or said about Lawrence. People have been terribly eager to point out his faults before ever they allowed themselves to recognise his qualities and achievements; and they've tried to explain him away long before they understood him. Like every creative man, Lawrence suffered from the hundreds of people who would like to create, and can't. The unconscious envy of this type disguises itself as 'critical standards', and its attack is always against the essentially creative and original artist.

I don't mean that Lawrence wasn't appreciated as a writer. From the Garnetts and Hueffer at the beginning, on to Aldous Huxley at the end, there were always distinguished men who admired him, as well as a growing number of silent people who bought his books. But how much there was against him! The Home Office with its policemen and beastly War-time spies; many of the reviewers; the huge stupid puritanical middle class; and all the nasty busybodies who are always so busy watching and warding other people's morals. It was a lot for a poor miner's son to fight, even though he was a great writer. I do think it is up to us to see that his courage and energy are not misrepresented and betrayed.

I often think that the biggest blow Lawrence ever received was the prosecution of *The Rainbow*. They can say all they like about 'obscenity', but you and I know in our bones that the real reason for the attack was that he denounced War. And you were German, so of course Lawrence was plotting to bring the Prussian Guards into Cornwall in submarines. Probably only you know how much he suffered in those War years, though other people can guess if they will read the 'Nightmare' chapters in *Kangaroo*. I think it was the utter stupid misjudging of him, and the complete betrayal by nearly everyone who ought to have stood by him, which hurt him, far more than the bitter poverty which the prosecution brought. As if he did not care far more for England than the 'patriotic' fools and knaves who ruined it for us! For the War was a triumph of that evil hatred of life which he always struggled against.

His acceptance of the poverty was one of the sweet things in him. You remember the time after you were both turned out of Cornwall as dangerous conspirators, and afterwards went to live at that little cottage of Margaret Radford's at Hermitage. He described it all in *Kangaroo*—how poor you were, and how you often hadn't enough to eat, and how he went out in the evening to gather the woodcutters' chips so that you could have a fire. The trees were being cut down to further the ends of the destructionists, so it was only right that the man who believed in life and creativeness should have only the chips. He writes about all that with a simple-hearted acceptance which is deeply touching, because it is so unconscious. The resentment in him was not about his own suffering or even yours, but at the triumph of the world's yahoos over the human beings.

The way people misunderstand all this is rather exasperating. In the summer of 1930 I received a letter (one of those hoity-toity superior letters which people think they have a right to send because they've spent a few shillings on a book) from a man, a schoolmaster I think he was, about my little book on Lawrence. This man said I was quite wrong to protest—he knew Lawrence was popular, because two of his friends were Lawrence enthusiasts, and he knew he had plenty of money because Lawrence first editions fetched as much as three pounds! Doesn't it make you cross? That little book was published in America in 1927 (nobody would issue it in England until after Lawrence was dead, and therefore famous) and, as you know, he was never without money anxiety until 1928, and then it was too late. I remember at the Mirenda in 1926, you were both so pleased because he had got £80 for a short story from the *Saturday Evening Post*—very pleasant, except that I knew they then paid anything from £100 to £500 to other far less gifted writers.

You know how simply he lived, how completely without any sort of extravagance, how unmercenary his writing was, how he even gave away manuscripts, and how cross he was with me at Port-Cros for trying to make him more 'business-like'. So you will hardly believe it when I tell you that somebody recently informed me that 'Lawrence loved money'. We shall hear next that he loved power and had political ambitions. Naturally, a hungry man is pleased when he gets some food; and it does not surprise me that a man should be pleased to have a little money after being poor for forty years. I don't call that 'loving money'. To hear people talk you might suppose he had yachts and had Hispano-Suizas and large villas at Cannes. I remember once at Port-Cros we were all making out the list of provisions. Lawrence wanted a whole ham, and you said it would be too expensive; and he said, very proudly and extravagantly, 'Never mind, we've got £700—let's have what we want.' So we got the 'money-lover' his ham!

The absurd popular Lawrence-legend reaches me in forms which do not come to you. All sorts of little episodes, which showed the utterly false ideas circulating about him, come into my memory. There was the well-meaning but sadly stupid literary gentleman, who gravely informed me that Lawrence was 'one of the most sinister figures of our time'. Only last year I heard a wealthy middle-class woman say at a party, 'Lawrence? He's the man who hates women, isn't he?' Perhaps one should pay no attention to such idiocies, but they annoy me. I hope the books that you and his sister are bringing out will destroy some of these ill-natured calumnies; but, though truth is great, it seems to take a long while to prevail. I think Ada Lawrence is quite right when she says that nowadays our rulers underhandedly try to discredit and ruin a man whose ideas do not please them, instead of adopting the more direct methods of their ancestors, such as burning and imprisonment.

In the last twenty years other writers have been banned or persecuted, but Lawrence was peculiarly unlucky, or shall we say, selected. There is something very irritating in the back-stairs methods now so much favoured in England. A writer may be secretly denounced by his rivals, and is judged and condemned by his inferiors. I know that in France during the War I received a communication from some English Vice Society, asking for a subscription to carry on their good work and boasting that their latest achievement was—what do you think?—the suppression of *Rainbow*. I lost the document, but I remember that it was signed (among others) by a Bishop and a 'literary critic' now dead. Another and more startling example of animosity towards Lawrence came my way once when I was on leave, and staying in the same house with you both. When everybody else was out I discovered a man poking about the house, and he informed me that he was a detective sent to investigate Lawrence's activities in London. (It sounds a bit mad, but it's true.) I tried to point out that Lawrence had neither the will nor the means to do any material harm to the Allied and Associated Powers, and that his attitude towards the War was determined by moral and human considerations. This, however, went rather over his head. Reassured by my uniform, he became quite confidential, and finally informed me that he had read some of Lawrence's books and 'didn't fink much of 'em'.

From this distance, it seems comic, particularly when you know that our treasonable activities the night before had been limited to playing charades under Lawrence's direction. (How he bossed us about, as if we were children, and insisted on having the most important part himself!) But at that time it was more serious and tragic than we realised. All this opposition and persecution and calumny (which in his case was certainly greater than the normal hostility every original writer must expect) made him feel very lonely. The 'intellectuals' let him down as badly as anybody. From 1916 to about 1921 Lawrence felt, and indeed almost was, a pariah. And the result was not only the desperate feeling so startlingly expressed in *Kangaroo*, but a sharpness and intolerance very unlike his own genuine sweetness and charm. In this very *Apocalypse*, to which I am leading up, you will find him snapping at sun-bathers for lying on the beach 'like pigs'.

His ordinary rages and crossnesses had nothing to do with this later sharpness which I was surprised to find in him after you came back from Mexico. (I did not see him between 1919 and 1926, and so noticed such things.) In working-class homes people let off steam much more freely than in bourgeois homes, where a sort of rancour often lurks under the superficial good manners. Very likely Lawrence was only doing what he had seen his father do a thousand times—work off his annoyance by shouting and apparently unnecessary violence. But with these people, once the scene is over, there is no ill-will at all. Everybody has worked off his or her annoyance, and is quite prepared to be affectionate again. People like ourselves are brought up to conceal our feelings; he always expressed his. Once I had worked that out for myself, I didn't at all mind his occasional crossnesses; but I did mind that sharp girding at so many people and things. Yet I believe it was not inherent in his nature. It was created in him by the spirit of persecution and hostility which met nearly everything he wrote. A little genuine effort to understand what he was trying to say, a slight gleam of intelligence in wooden-headed officials, would have spared him much humiliation and suffering. It was the humiliation he could not forgive. But I am indeed glad that he never wasted time in replying to literary 'attacks', that he made the only reply an artist need make —writing another fine book.

What annoyed, and still annoys me, is that Lawrence was attacked on 'moral' grounds by people who ought to have shut up when the word 'morality' was mentioned. For instance, there was one 'critic'—now deceased—whose hobby was the collection of filthy verses and writing indecent letters. And there is another whom I will not specify in any way. The beastly hypocrisy of it! These people hated Lawrence because he was a clean man, because he had such reverence and delight in the beauty and glory of sex and sex-love, that he would not endure anything which degraded or sneered at them. Do you remember how our Italian friend, G., used to say laughingly, 'How moral they are, those Lawrences, how moral!' But it was true. I think Lawrence had the sweetest imagination and feeling about sex of any man I have known; just as, in its essential meaning, he was a truly 'religious' man.

It isn't necessary for me to insist any further on this, since you and his sister are writing about him. I hope you'll give the quietus to all the highbrow and lowbrow calumnies—particularly the highbrow ones. But I must add one little story to show how sensitive Lawrence was to anything which he thought at all vulgar or indelicate in these matters. One day we were spelling out Etruscan inscriptions—you know, they go from right to left. I transcribed a, r, s, e. Lawrence scratched his head and said, 'I wonder what that means, Richard?' I said, 'Well, I don't know what it means in Etruscan, but I know what it means in English.' How cross he was with me! Afterwards he said to someone else, 'You know, I used to think Richard was sound, but now I'm afraid he's just like other Englishmen!'

I mustn't prolong these reminiscences, because this, after all, is meant to be an introduction to *Apocalypse*, yet I can't help giving one more glimpse of this *wicked* man. It was at the Mirenda. You had gone into Florence to do some shopping, and Lawrence and I sat in deck-chairs under the chestnut trees at the back of the villa. The October afternoon was very warm and golden, and we talked about this and that, and occasionally a ripe chestnut slipped out of its bulging spiky burr and plopped in the grass. Our real interest was not in talking, but in the children of the contadini. Every now and then, a shy little barefoot child would come stealing through the bushes with a bunch of grapes. Lawrence would say, 'Look! There's another. Pretend not to see.' The child would come very stealthily forward over the grass, like a little animal, and then stop and gaze at him. Finally, Lawrence would look up, and say with a pretence of surprise, 'Che vuoi?' 'Niente, Signor Lorenzo.' 'Viene qui.' Then the child would come up very shyly, and present the grapes. 'Ma, cosa hai li?' 'Uva, Signor Lorenzo.' 'Per me?' 'Sissignore.' 'Come ti chiami?' And then was a grand scene, trying to make out the child's name. We were

terribly puzzled by "'stasio', until we decided it must be
'Anastasio'. But every time, Lawrence, ill as he was, went
into the house to get the child a piece of chocolate, or some
sugar when all the chocolate was gone. And each time he
apologised to me for his generosity (for at Vendemmia, as
you know, grapes are worth nothing, and chocolate and
sugar are always expensive luxuries) by telling me how
poor the peasants were, and how the children ought to
have sugar for the sake of their health.

And in England they called him 'a sewer'. Per Bacco!

It is sometimes suggested that Lawrence made himself
unpopular by 'putting people in his books', and there is
Norman Douglas's pamphlet about Lawrence and Maurice
Magnus in support of this view. Now, I'm not one of those
clever people who know what went on in Shakespeare's
mind when he wrote *Hamlet* and in Keats's when he wrote
the *Nightingale*. So I shan't pretend that I can tell you what
went on in Lawrence's mind when he wrote his novels and
poems and essays. If you think about his books, you will
see that they form a whole; and that it is a vast imaginative
spiritual autobiography. Lawrence believed that you cannot
write about anything but yourself, by which I suppose he
meant that a writer must keep within the limits of his
experience. He also said that the writing of a book is an
adventure of the mind. Lawrence made use of traits of
character, situations, relationships among the people he
knew. But he used these imaginatively, and very often
merely to project his own inner experience.

This Norman Douglas denounces as 'the novelist's touch',
asserting that such writing at its best is a travesty of life,
at its worst dishonest. And he proceeds to show that the
Magnus he knew was not at all the person described by
Lawrence. But a poet is not bound to the literal accuracy
of a biologist. Oddly enough, this Magnus book contains
some of Lawrence's most beautiful descriptive prose.
It seems plain to me that what Lawrence wrote was a short
imaginative novel about a possible (not necessarily the real)
Magnus, and that his grave error was to publish this as a
biography. As I knew nothing of Magnus, I can easily read
the thing as a short novel, and as such I find it extremely
interesting. Thus, while I believe Douglas was right to con-
demn what he thought was a travesty of his friend, I think

he was wrong to extend his condemnation to Lawrence's avowed fiction. Otherwise the contemporary novel becomes impossible, and every doctor's wife in Normandy will be taking action against the author of a future *Madame Bovary*. In any case, I do not think that the resentment of persons who imagined that he had written about them unflatteringly in his novels was responsible for the fantastic legendary Lawrence and the hostility to his books; though, doubtless, such people would not always strive too officiously to defend him.

I have tried to give with frankness my own impression of the man whom you knew far more intimately than anybody else. Before I go on to talk about *Apocalypse* I must try to tell you what is my explanation of the anger and hostility at his books, a hostility which spread from them to himself, and made of him in common imaginations such a monster that there is scarcely any relation between the Lawrence we knew and the Lawrence of the Press and common talk. I shall take only a few simple and fairly obvious points, for I am not such a fool as to imagine that I can explain all Lawrence in a preface.

There was nothing particularly surprising or remarkable in his shocking the circulating library public. It is the most omnivorous public in existence, interested in everything except literature and life, from which it is conscientiously defended on all fronts. The prussic-aciders are always with us. The official prosecution arose out of War panic (supported by a little virtue) and was prolonged by mere departmental stupidity—which did not make it any more endurable or any less reprehensible on the part of those responsible. You will see at once what I mean when I say that offence was given all round, not by any sort of scandalous behaviour or horridness of character in him, but by his whole attitude towards human life and human beings. I believe Lawrence had a great deal of love in him, and the sharpness I have regretted only came after his love had been grotesquely misunderstood and flung back at him as hatred. I intend to write this without dragging in Jesus, so I will put it in this way: suppose a Nietzsche who effected a transvaluation not of intellectual values, but of fundamental human values. Such was Lawrence. And he paid the price.

Before Lawrence, the primacy of the intellect had been

doubted by Bergson, the psychology of the unconscious had been formulated by Freud, and the whole system of values of European civilization had been rejected in their different ways by Tolstoy and Nietzsche, and even Dostoievsky. Lawrence differs from them, partly because he was English, but chiefly because he was essentially a poet—a poet who for various reasons found his more effective medium was prose. But, being an Englishman of his class and time, he could scarcely avoid being a preacher as well as a poet. It was the preacher who brought the house down on his own head. From the point of view of the intellectuals (and this is the reason why they treated him either with coldness or hostility) Lawrence's fundamental heresy was simply that he placed quality of feelings, intensity of sensations and passion before intellect. In this he is the very antithesis of Bernard Shaw, a fanatic of the intellect, who was at the height of his powers and influence when Lawrence began writing. See the complete contrast between the optimistic belief of the Fabians that anything and everything could be achieved by the human intellect, and Lawrence's conviction that intellect is a dangerous, even pernicious thing which leads only to death.

Perhaps I put this a little too strongly, and in any case I must insist that he felt and wrote about these things as a poet, and not as a philosopher with a system to expound. I think you will agree that what Lawrence had to give and wanted to give was a new or different way of feeling, living, and loving, and not a new way of thinking. You cannot put him into formulas. Of course, he had to think too— how else could he be a writer? But his problem as a writer was to put into words these feelings and perceptions which he believed to be independent of the conscious intellect. This was difficult enough for Lawrence, who was dealing with his own experience; it is almost impossible for anyone else, who may entirely misinterpret what he wrote. For example, what exactly were the experiences expressed (or rather, symbolised) in those beautiful but curious poems in *The Plumed Serpent*? What did he mean when he spoke of the Indian singing as 'mindless'? What exactly are the 'physical life' and the 'tenderness' he used to talk to us about? I can feel, you can feel what he meant, but they are not things which can be pinned down with neat defining sentences. These things cannot be expressed except through images and symbols and the evocative descriptions at which Lawrence excelled.

This rejection of the sovereignty of the intellect is the cause of much of the misunderstanding and hostility Lawrence endured. It made him look like a crank, and thereby estranged the intellectuals. At the same time, his rejection of organised religion naturally offended the enormous number of people who are still enthralled by it. The so-called 'spiritual' values had no interest for him at all; and numerous idiots went about saying that Lawrence wished us to become 'animal' or even 'amœbic'. Finally, he was serious about sexual love. There are all sorts of accepted attitudes towards sex, which you can get away with because *au fond* they all imply contempt and disgust, the Pauline conviction that sexual desire is base, impure and sinful. You may be sentimental-pure or sentimental-prurient, mocking or solemn, materialist or idealist, sociological or medical; but you may not say (and believe and experience) that sexual desire is a glorious and beautiful thing. Any other god may be worshipped, but not *Æneidum genetrix, hominum divumque voluptas*. (That 'voluptas' is the crime—why, a skilful journalist very nearly shook the English superstition about Shakespeare by suggesting that the Bard was 'a voluptuary'.) Thus while Lawrence informed mankind that they were scarcely living at all, they retorted by calling him a cretin, a sewer, and a pornographist. A sad imbroglio.

Towards the end of his life Lawrence wrote three books which are very important towards an understanding of him. They are *The Man Who Died*, the essays on Etruscan Towns, and—most important of all—*Apocalypse*. The Etruscan book had been in his mind for a long time, and he died without finishing it. I thought the manuscript (it has not yet been published) extremely interesting, less perhaps for what it told me about the Etruscans (though that is stimulating enough) than for what it told me about Lawrence. To put it roughly in a sentence, Lawrence believed that the Etruscans of about 700—300 B.C. had lived largely in the way he wished to live and thought that we should all live. The Etruscans were a great convenience, for, since nobody knows much about them, nobody could contradict what he said. Lawrence ranged pretty far both in space and time in search of other modes of living which could be used either as symbols for expressing his faith or as sticks to beat the moderns. He found bits of what he wanted in German and Italian peasants, in Mexicans and Indians. (You remember how he liked the fishermen at Lavandou, going out in boats with their sons, playing boules, and eating bouillabaisse with their wives? Alas, they are lost already among cocktail-drinking tourists and ladies in trousers.)

These traces of elemental life were not enough for him. In Europe they are being obliterated every day, and probably even more rapidly in America. Moreover, I think he grew dissatisfied with his savages, if only because (as he says somewhere) their consciousness is so different from ours that there is scarcely any possibility of communication. The white man can do nothing with the savage except to destroy or enslave, since it is too much to expect the elementary justice of leaving him alone. Lawrence's return to Tuscany was fortunate. I think he always liked it, and was as happy at the Mirenda as anywhere, except perhaps the Ranch and Sicily. Boccaccio, who is the very essence of country Tuscany, was one of the few authors he always loved, a man filled with that warm instinctive life Lawrence wanted so much to see around him. And for a long time he had had a hankering to investigate the Etruscans for himself, and to write a book about them.

The Etruscans were quite a godsend. Here was a lost European civilization which had never been guilty of a Homer or a Plato, had indeed no extant literature at all. There is no history of the Etruscans, for the book about them by the Emperor Claudius has disappeared, and the dislike of the Romans for a conquered and perhaps more civilised people, added to Christian horror of 'pagans', has left us little but archæology and conjecture. To increase their attractiveness, you will find that the Etruscans are not favourites with the learned, who accuse them of immorality and of borrowing what culture they had from other races. They were a very religious people, greatly interested in the divine significance of the flight of birds and of the entrails of sacrifices. They must have believed in some sort of life after death, since they constructed cities of elaborate tombs (planned in imitation of their towns), burying their dead in full armour or festival robes in painted chambers filled with precious objects and offerings to the dead. Sometimes the dead were burned, and placed in carved marble or alabaster coffers.

Lawrence believed that Etruscan art had a quality of its own, quite different from Greek or Roman art; and what he found there and liked so much was that intense 'physical' life he thought the world has very nearly lost. The Etruscans did not possess much 'æsthetic' feeling, the Greek love of perfection, harmony, grace. They were wonderful craftsmen in gold, for the best modern goldsmiths cannot quite equal the delicacy of their filigree work. The best of their bronzes have great spirit and energy—for example, the chariot and shields in the Vatican, and the elongated statuettes in Florence. The Apollo of Veii at the Villa di Papa Giulio and the tomb in the British Museum show what they could achieve in terracotta. Almost more important are the wall-paintings and the carved stone caskets of the dead. On or near every Etruscan tomb was a conventionalised phallus—a symbol of the triumph of life over death. Some of the later wall-paintings have horrid devils of death in them, but most of the earlier ones are rather gay. They depict the life of the living, and there are real warmth and tenderness in the love-scenes. Moreover, those carved figures of obese magistrates and often ugly men and women have extraordinary vitality. They fascinate an attentive observer, in Rome and Florence, in Volterra, Perugia, Orvieto—even in the smallest collection.

All this you know as well as I; but the point I want to stress is the depth to which Lawrence was stirred by these vestiges of a lost civilisation. For my present purpose, it is quite irrelevant to ask whether Lawrence had or had not any 'scientific' basis for Etruscan enthusiasm. What matters is that he found in the Etruscans (or lent them, it doesn't matter) a conception of life such as he believed in himself. Perhaps it is only a poet's dream, a transference to the remote past of an ideal he despaired of finding in the present. This conception comes up again in *Apocalypse*, and indeed runs through much of his work. In *Apocalypse* the Etruscans have fallen into the background, as rather belated specimens of the 'great Ægean civilisation' which existed before 1000 B.C., of which the Etruscans are quite possibly an off-shoot. Whether imagined or not, here at least were civilisations which Lawrence felt he could love, nations of men and women living an intense 'physical' life without too much restless intellect and hatred. And in Etruria at any rate the women enjoyed great liberty and consideration, while the idea of sex and sexual desire as shameful things had never been thought of—that was an importation of the puritan Romans.

I shall only say a little about *The Man Who Died*. It is intensely personal, and the saddest thing Lawrence ever wrote. It is the only thing in his work which looks like a confession of defeat, and this he promptly countered by writing *Apocalypse*. The opening part when he describes the mingled agony and gradual happiness in creeping back from death to life is full of pathos; one can't help thinking of his own sufferings as he recovered from one or other of his serious crises. Like much of Lawrence's writing, it has more than one meaning. You can take it as an expression of his latest feelings about Jesus—a rejection of Jesus as a teacher, an acceptance of Jesus as the lover. The mistake of Jesus was not in loving, but in trying to influence men by a doctrine of love. Even when he was struggling with the problem of love and hatred, Lawrence was always a great lover; his deepest and most passionate belief was in love. It was because he loved so much that he also hated so intensely all the enemies of love. But that forlorn, lonely suffering creature just shivering back to life in the sun outside the peasant's hut is also a symbol of Lawrence himself. In this mood of agonised convalescence he doubted his own life. He did not doubt love, for the triumph of love is still his theme, but he doubted both the love he had given to mankind in general and all his own efforts as a writer. It would have been better, he seems to imply, just to live out a life of love, and not to try to give love to all. Isn't it true that he was misunderstood and sneered at by those he was trying to illuminate with his love, and even that he was betrayed? If I read this story correctly, then it expresses the bitterest moments of Lawrence's life. How glad I am that he lived to write *Apocalypse*!

In several of Lawrence's novels we see the conflict between this mysterious 'dark consciousness', this 'sense-awareness', and the 'intellectual' consciousness of the modern world, which he felt was utterly hostile and destructive to the other and (for him) deeper and more vital way of living. There, he used human characters as symbols. In *Apocalypse* he uses strange primitive symbols, such as you find in pre-Christian art and, oddly enough, in the Book of Revelation. *Apocalypse* is a kind of last testament, a last effort to make himself understood by the very many who had either not listened to him or had failed to understand him. The despair of *The Man Who Died* has disappeared, and it is significant that he could not help trying just once more to do something for the humanity he so obviously loved if only because he scolded it so much. *Apocalypse* is essentially a book of hope and life, although it condemns so completely *all* our contemporary ways of living.

I've tried to show how this study of the Etruscans had stimulated his interest in early civilisations; and this study must have revived an interest in symbols which so far as I know he always had. And, I repeat, *The Man Who Died* is a rejection of Jesus the teacher, though not of Jesus the lover. But in *Apocalypse* Lawrence not only comes out as an interpreter of strange old symbols, but as a teacher and a lover—he could not put off his nature so easily. If he had really ceased to care about men and women, he would have ceased to write; or, at any rate, he would not have written a book like *Apocalypse*, which attempts to give ordinary people the clue to the kind of life he felt he had discovered. I doubt if he was entirely happy with his red and green dragons and beasts with starry wings and coloured horses. You know he admitted to you that he was a little bored by them, which was very endearing of him, for they are a trifle boring in the end.

From the point of view of scholars Lawrence's book may be quite worthless as an interpretation of the Book of Revelation. That is neither here nor there, at least so far as I am concerned. *Apocalypse* interests me not as the revelation of John of Patmos, but as the revelation of Lawrence. The things he says by the way are more valuable than the interpretation, whatever it may be worth. In *Apocalypse* he goes further (I think) than in any of his other books, except perhaps in *Mornings in Mexico*. Here we are quite definitely told that this different 'consciousness' he was always talking about, this different 'sense-awareness', this life of man 'breast to breast with the cosmos', can only exist in its plenitude outside what he calls our 'cycle', the cycle of Platonic 'spiritual' philosophy, of Christianity and of science. This 'cosmos' he talks of is a 'living thing' with which man may commune and which will commune with him:

'We and the cosmos are one. The cosmos is a vast living body, of which we are still parts. The sun is a great heart whose tremors run through our smallest veins. The moon is a great gleaming nerve-centre from which we quiver forever.'

But:

'We have lost the cosmos. The sun strengthens us no more, neither does the moon.'

And that was because 'the old vital religions' were rejected by 'intellectuals' like Aristotle and all who derive from him and by the Christians:

'The cosmos became anathema to the Christians, though the early Catholic Church restored it somewhat after the crash of the Dark Ages. Then again the cosmos became anathema to the Protestants after the Reformation. They substituted the non-vital universe of forces and mechanistic order, everything else became abstraction, and the long slow death of the human being set in. This slow death produced science and machinery, but both are death products.'

I like the distinction between science and machinery, because to many persons science is the machine; when they talk of the 'marvels of modern science' they mean airplanes and wireless and electric light. But machinery is only a by-product of true science, which is the search for an abstract something called the Truth. But since 'the Truth' does not exist, Lawrence, like Remy de Gourmont before him, is quite justified in calling it a death-product. This cult for 'Truth', the most abstract of kakodaimons, withers the vital impulses, so that mankind is reduced to the pitiable belief that we live by bread alone—taking bread as symbolical of commodities. To this lie, which is indeed a lie in the soul, Lawrence cried, 'Better lack bread than lack life.'

Thus I believe that *Apocalypse* perfectly rounds off the long series of Lawrence's writings, is a splendid valediction. It protests against the dehumanising of men and women by Christianity, which promises them an imaginary heaven after they are dead, 'if they are good'. And it protests against their dehumanising by 'science', which has taken the gods out of heaven and the heart out of men. And by implication it protests against the puerile conceptions of men like Bernard Shaw, with their ridiculous tyrannical 'organisations' and equal incomes. As if life were a matter of income! It may be said (though you will not say it) that the experience behind *Apocalypse*—or rather the conception of life and consciousness expressed in the book—is a purely mystic one. Well, we can all argue that the experiences we have not had are invalid or non-existent. But Rousseau experienced this same physical ecstasy, this same sensation of living 'breast to breast with the cosmos' when he was living in the Ile de Saint-Pierre. All his life afterwards was a regret for this lost 'consciousness' (for he lost it when he had to leave the island) and an attempt to regain it.

If people try to read *Apocalypse* either as a work of scholarship or of scientific analysis, they make a mistake, for it is nothing of the kind. Lawrence makes use of the book to illustrate a double theme. He shows that it embodies the 'Christianity' of the uneducated under-dog dissenting sort of Christian because it is the expression of frustrated power-lust. Parallel with this he ventures on the bolder assertion that much of the symbolism is taken from very ancient and pre-Christian cosmogonies, conceptions of man and the universe which the Christians meant to destroy and did destroy but whose symbolism they used because human consciousness was still saturated by it, and because they could not invent another themselves, or at best only in part.

The two themes are interwoven with all Lawrence's astonishing literary skill. For him, it is a comparatively cool book with little of that passionate eloquence which came to him so naturally when he was deeply moved; but, obviously, he was keeping himself under strict control. The remarkable thing is that a book by a dying man should contain so much energy, physical energy. The glow and warmth of himself, as of his very blood and flesh, which Lawrence gave in his books, are wonderful and a lovable thing. There was no literary posing, no dry crackle of witticism, no arid friendless mind-spinning in his work. It was himself. He could have echoed Whitman truly, for who touches Lawrence's books touches a man. Yet *Apocalypse* is the book of a dying man, and you might think it would have to be excused as such. Not a bit. The rich passion, the lovely poetic sensual imagination are a little muted, because this differs from nearly all Lawrence's other books. It is a work of exposition rather than of creation, though it is created; it is an attempt to explain his beliefs, rather than to embody them in a work of art. But it is a living book. And it is not about death, but about life.

How easy it all looks to an outsider, and what exquisite writing-power is behind these easy almost colloquial sentences! From the very beginning you feel, you must feel, the old fascinating Lawrence spell. He starts so quietly, just making you realise his own boyhood, and how his child consciousness was saturated with the Bible words until his mind rejected them with loathing. He moves outward from himself, and takes us into the cold ugly miners' chapels with the flaring gas-jets and the voice roaring out the denunciations of John of Patmos against the rich and the splendid and the lovely and the powerful—all the magnificent things of life they hadn't got and wanted so much and envied, but especially the power. And then the writing sweeps out in wider and wider circles, like a swift hawk soaring round and round and higher, just as he would talk when he was in the right mood. He shows how this envy of power, this desire for the utter destruction of Babylon the Great, the symbol of all the splendid power and magnificence of the world, so that in the end the weak under-dogs are left as the only rulers—how this gospel of hate has slipped into the gospel of love, was bound to do so, since it is always the religion of the have-nots.

The religion of Jesus (not the religion of John of Patmos), he says, is a religion for individuals. It is not (he maintains) a religion for the collective side of man's nature, which needs more than love. Men need to identify themselves with a splendid hierarchy, to feel themselves fulfilled in 'their' Emperor or King and 'their' nobles. (This curious piece of English snobbery might be a justification of the Church of Rome—a consequence of his argument which Lawrence does not appear to have noticed.) And so through the long analysis of the 'old symbolists' and their cosmogonies, which

I have already mentioned, Lawrence leads up to a sort of credo which is well worth meditating, even by those who are hostile to Lawrence. His six points are elaborated, but briefly they are:

(1) No man can be a pure individual.
(2) The State, or what we call society as a collective whole, cannot have the psychology of an individual.
(3) The State cannot be Christian.
(4) Every citizen is a unit of worldly power.
(5) As a citizen, as a collective being, man has his fulfilment in the gratification of his power-sense.
(6) To have an ideal for the individual which regards only his individual self and ignores his collective self is in the long run fatal.

Thus baldly summarised, these sound as if *Apocalypse* petered out into a political tract of Six Points for the Continuance of War. But I am not concerned to argue that now. For me the interesting part of *Apocalypse* is its 'poetic' side, and I do not mind whether poets hold sound theories of political world-organisation, or not. At any rate, Lawrence's dream is of a *human* world, and the aim and spirit of the book is the attainment of abounding life. And he concludes with a magnificent passage, such as only he could write, which I throw as a refutation and a challenge to his enemies:

'What man most passionately wants is his living wholeness and his living unison, not his own isolate salvation of his "soul". Man wants his physical fulfilment first and foremost, since now, once and once only, he is in the flesh and potent. For man, the vast marvel is to be alive. For man, as for flower and beast and bird, the supreme triumph is to be most vividly, most perfectly alive. Whatever the unborn and the dead may know, they cannot know the beauty, the marvel of being alive in the flesh. The dead may look after the afterwards. But the magnificent here and now of life in the flesh is ours, and ours only for a time. We ought to dance with rapture that we should be alive and in the flesh, and part of the living, incarnate cosmos. I am part of the sun as my eye is part of me. That I am part of the earth my feet know perfectly, and my blood is part of the sea. My soul knows that I am part of the human race, my soul is an organic part of the great human soul, as my spirit is part of my nation.'

And so, dear Frieda, au revoir, with all good wishes to you, and all my reverence for the great English writer who was your husband.

RICHARD ALDINGTON

Apocalypse

CHAPTER I

APOCALYPSE means simply Revelation, though there is nothing simple about this one, since men have puzzled their brains for nearly two thousand years to find out what, exactly, is revealed in all its orgy of mystification, and of all the books in the Bible, they find Revelation perhaps the least attractive.

That is my own first feeling about it. From earliest years right into manhood, like any other nonconformist child I had the Bible poured every day into my helpless consciousness, till there came almost a saturation point. Long before one could think or even vaguely understand, this Bible language, these 'portions' of the Bible were *douched* over the mind and consciousness, till they became soaked in, they became an influence which affected all the processes of emotion and thought. So that today, although I have 'forgotten' my Bible, I need only begin to read a chapter to realise that I 'know' it with an almost nauseating fixity. And I must confess, my first reaction is one of dislike, repulsion, and even resentment. My very instincts *resent* the Bible.

The reason is now fairly plain to me. Not only was the Bible, in portions, poured into the childish consciousness day in, day out, year in, year out, willy-nilly, whether the consciousness could assimilate it or not, but also it was day in, day out, year in, year out expounded, dogmatically, and always morally expounded, whether it was in day-school or Sunday-school, at home or in Band of Hope or Christian Endeavour. The interpretation was always the same, whether it was a Doctor of Divinity in the pulpit, or the big blacksmith who was my Sunday-school teacher. Not only was the Bible verbally trodden into the consciousness, like innumerable foot-prints treading a surface hard, but the foot-prints were always mechanically alike, the interpretation was fixed, so that all real interest was lost.

The process defeats its own ends. While the Jewish poetry penetrates the emotions and the imagination, and the Jewish morality penetrates the instincts, the mind becomes stubborn, resistant, and at last repudiates the whole Bible authority, and turns with a kind of repugnance away from the Bible altogether. And this is the condition of many men of my generation.

Now a book lives as long as it is unfathomed. Once it is fathomed, it dies at once. It is an amazing thing, how utterly different a book will be, if I read it again after five years. Some books gain immensely, they are a new thing. They are so astonishingly different, they make a man question his own identity. Again, other books lose immensely. I read *War and Peace* once more, and was amazed to find how little it moved me, I was almost aghast to think of the raptures I had once felt, and now felt no more.

So it is. Once a book is fathomed, once it is *known*, and its meaning is fixed or established, it is dead. A book only lives while it has power to move us, and move us *differently*; so long as we find it *different* every time we read it. Owing to the flood of shallow books which really are exhausted in one reading, the modern mind tends to think every book is the same, finished in one reading. But it is not so. And gradually the modern mind will realise it again. The real joy of a book lies in reading it over and over again, and always finding it different, coming upon another meaning, another level of meaning. It is, as usual, a question of values: we are so overwhelmed with *quantities* of books, that we hardly realise any more that a book can be valuable, valuable like a jewel, or a lovely picture, into which you can look deeper and deeper and get a more profound experience every time. It is far, far better to read one book six times, at intervals, than to read six several books. Because if a certain book can call you to read it six times, it will be a deeper and deeper experience each time, and will enrich the whole soul, emotional and mental. Whereas six books read once only are merely an accumulation of superficial interest, the burdensome accumulation of modern days, quantity without real value.

We shall now see the reading public dividing again into two groups: the vast mass, who read for amusement and for momentary interest, and the small minority, who only want the books which have value to themselves, books which yield experience, and still deeper experience.

The Bible is a book that has been temporarily killed for us, or for some of us, by having its meaning arbitrarily fixed. We know it so thoroughly, in its superficial or popular meaning, that it is dead, it gives us nothing any more. Worse still, by old habit amounting almost to instinct, it imposes on us a whole state of feeling which is now repugnant to us. We detest the 'chapel' and the Sunday-school feeling which the Bible must necessarily impose on us. We want to get rid of all that *vulgarity*—for vulgarity it is.

Perhaps the most detestable of all these books of the Bible, taken superficially, is Revelation. By the time I was ten, I am sure I had heard, and read, that book ten times over, even without knowing or taking real heed. And without ever knowing or thinking about it, I am sure it always roused in me a real dislike. Without realising it, I must, from earliest childhood, have detested the pie-pie mouthing, solemn, portentous, loud way in which everybody read the Bible, whether it was parsons or teachers or ordinary persons. I dislike the 'parson' voice through and through my bones. And this voice, I remember, was always at its worst when mouthing out some portion of Revelation. Even the phrases that still fascinate me I cannot recall without shuddering, because I can still hear the portentous declamation of a nonconformist clergyman: 'And I saw heaven opened, and behold a white horse; and he that sat upon him was called——' there my memory suddenly stops, deliberately blotting out the next words: 'Faithful and True.' I hated, even as a child, allegory: people having the names of mere qualities, like this somebody on a white horse, called 'Faithful and True'. In the same way I could never read *Pilgrim's Progress*. When as a small boy I learnt from Euclid that: 'The whole is greater than the part,' I immediately knew that that solved the problem of allegory for me. A man is more than mere Faithfulness and Truth, and when people are merely personifications of qualities they cease to be people for me. Though as a young man I almost loved Spenser and his *Faerie Queene*, I had to gulp at his allegory.

But the Apocalypse is, and always was from earliest childhood, to me antipathetic. In the first place its splendi-

ferous imagery is distasteful because of its complete unnaturalness. 'And before the throne there was a sea of glass
like unto crystal: and in the midst of the throne, and
round about the throne, were four beasts full of eyes before
and behind.

'And the first beast was like a lion, and the second beast
like a calf, and the third beast had a face as a man, and
the fourth beast was like a flying eagle.

'And the four beasts had each of them six wings about
him; and they were full of eyes within: and they rest not
day and night, saying, Holy, holy, holy, Lord God Almighty,
which was, and is, and is to come.'

A passage like that irritated and annoyed my boyish
mind because of its pompous unnaturalness. If it is imagery,
it is imagery which cannot be imagined: for how can four
beasts be 'full of eyes before and behind', and how can they
be 'in the midst of the throne, and round about the throne'?
They can't be somewhere and somewhere else at the same
time. But that is how the Apocalypse is.

Again, much of the imagery is utterly unpoetic and
arbitrary, some of it really ugly, like all the wadings in
blood, and the rider's shirt dipped in blood, and people
washen in the blood of the Lamb. Also such phrases as 'the
wrath of the Lamb' are on the face of them ridiculous. But
this is the grand phraseology and imagery of the nonconformist chapels, all the Bethels of England and America,
and all the Salvation armies. And vital religion is said to be
found, in all ages, down among the uneducated people.

Down among the uneducated people you will still find
Revelation rampant. I think it has had, and perhaps still has
more influence, actually, than the Gospels or the great
Epistles. The huge denunciation of Kings and Rulers, and of
the whore that sitteth upon the waters is entirely sympa-
thetic to a Tuesday evening congregation of colliers and
colliers' wives, on a black winter night, in the great barn-
like Pentecost Chapel. And the capital letters of the name:
MYSTERY, BABYLON THE GREAT, THE MOTHER OF HARLOTS
AND ABOMINATIONS OF THE EARTH thrill the old colliers today
as they thrilled the Scotch Puritan peasants and the more
ferocious of the early Christians. To the underground early
Christians, Babylon the great meant Rome, the great city
and the great empire which persecuted them. And great

was the satisfaction of denouncing her and bringing her to utter, utter woe and destruction, with all her kings, her wealth and her lordliness. After the Reformation, Babylon was once more identified with Rome, but this time it meant the Pope, and in Protestant and nonconformist England and Scotland out rolled the denunciations of John the Divine, with the grand cry: 'Babylon the great is fallen, is fallen, and is become the habitation of devils, and the hold of every foul spirit, and a cage of every unclean and hateful bird.' Nowadays the words are still mouthed out, and sometimes still they are hurled at the Pope and the Roman Catholics, who seem to be lifting their heads up again. But more often, today, Babylon means the rich and wicked people who live in luxury and harlotry somewhere in the vague distance, London, New York, or Paris worst of all, and who never once set foot in 'chapel', all their lives.

It is very nice, if you are poor and *not* humble—and the poor may be obsequious, but they are almost *never* truly humble in the Christian sense—to bring your grand enemies down to utter destruction and discomfiture, while you yourself rise up to grandeur. And nowhere does this happen so splendiferously as in Revelation. The great enemy in the eyes of Jesus was the Pharisee, harping on the letter of the law. But the Pharisee is too remote and subtle for the collier and the factory-worker. The Salvation Army at the street corner rarely raves about Pharisees. It raves about the Blood of the Lamb, and Babylon, Sion, and Sinners, the great harlot, and angels that cry Woe, Woe, Woe! and Vials that pour out horrible plagues. And above all, about being Saved, and sitting on the Throne with the Lamb, and reigning in Glory, and having Everlasting Life, and living in a grand city made of jasper, with gates of pearl: a city that 'had no need of the sun, neither of the moon, to shine in it'. If you listen to the Salvation Army you will hear that they are going to be very grand. Very grand indeed, since they get to heaven. *Then* they'll show you what's what. *Then* you'll be put in your place, you superior person, you Babylon: down in hell and in brimstone.

This is entirely the tone of Revelation. What we realise when we have read the precious book a few times is that John the Divine had on the face of it a grandiose scheme for wiping out and annihilating everybody who wasn't of the

elect, the chosen people, in short, and of climbing up himself right on to the throne of God. With nonconformity,
the chapel people took over to themselves the Jewish idea
of the chosen people. They were 'it', the elect, or the 'saved'.
And they took over the Jewish idea of ultimate triumph
and reign of the chosen people. From being bottom dogs
they were going to be top dogs: in Heaven. If not sitting
actually on the throne, they were going to sit in the lap of the
enthroned Lamb. It is doctrine you can hear any night from
the Salvation Army or in any Bethel or Pentecost Chapel.
If it is not Jesus, it is John. If it is not Gospel, it is Revelation. It is popular religion, as distinct from thoughtful
religion.

CHAPTER II

Or at least, it was popular religion when I was a boy. And I remember, as a child, I used to wonder over the curious sense of self-glory which one felt in the uneducated leaders, the men especially of the Primitive Methodist Chapels. They were not on the whole pious or mealy-mouthed or objectionable, these colliers who spoke heavy dialect and ran the 'Pentecost'. They certainly were not humble or apologetic. No, they came in from the pit and sat down to their dinners with a bang, and their wives and daughters ran to wait on them quite cheerfully, and their sons obeyed them without overmuch resentment. The home was rough yet not unpleasant, and there was an odd sense of wild mystery or power about, as if the chapel men really had some dispensation of rude power from above. Not love, but a rough and rather wild, somewhat 'special' sense of power. They were so *sure*, and as a rule their wives were quite humble to them. They ran a chapel, so they could run their household. I used to wonder over it, and rather enjoy it. But even I thought it rather 'common'. My mother, who was Congregationalist, never set foot in a Primitive Methodist Chapel in her life, I suppose. And she was certainly not prepared to be humble to her husband. If he'd been a real cheeky chapel man, she would no doubt have been much meeker with him. Cheek, that was the outstanding quality of chapel men. But a special kind of cheek, authorised from above, as it were. And I know now, a good deal of this special kind of religious cheek was backed up by the Apocalypse.

It was not till many years had gone by, and I had read something of comparative religion and the history of religion, that I realised what a strange book it was that had inspired the colliers on the black Tuesday nights in Pentecost or Beauvale Chapel to such a queer sense of

special authority and of religious cheek. Strange marvellous
black nights of the north Midlands, with the gas-light his-
sing in the chapel, and the roaring of the strong-voiced
colliers. Popular religion: a religion of self-glorification and
power, forever! and of darkness. No wailing 'Lead, kindly
Light!' about it.

The longer one lives, the more one realises that there
are two kinds of Christianity, the one focussed on Jesus and
the Command: Love one another!—and the other focussed,
not on Paul or Peter or John the Beloved, but on the Apocalypse. There is the Christianity of tenderness. But as far as
I can see, it is utterly pushed aside by the Christianity of
self-glorification: the self-glorification of the humble.

There's no getting away from it, mankind falls forever
into the two divisions of aristocrats and democrats. The
purest aristocrats during the Christian era have taught democracy. And the purest democrats try to turn themselves
into the most absolute aristocracy. Jesus was an aristocrat,
so was John the Apostle, and Paul. It takes a great aristocrat
to be capable of great tenderness and gentleness and un-
selfishness: the tenderness and gentleness of *strength*. From
the democrat you may often get the tenderness and gentleness of weakness: that's another thing. But you usually get
a sense of toughness.

We are speaking now not of political parties, but of the
two sorts of human nature: those that feel themselves
strong in their souls, and those that feel themselves weak.
Jesus and Paul and the greater John felt themselves strong.
John of Patmos felt himself weak, in his very soul.

In Jesus's day, the inwardly strong men everywhere had
lost their desire to rule on earth. They wished to withdraw
their strength from earthly rule and earthly power, and to
apply it to another form of life. Then the weak began to
rouse up and to feel *inordinately* conceited, they began to
express their rampant hate of the 'obvious' strong ones, the
men in worldly power.

So that religion, the Christian religion especially, became
dual. The religion of the strong taught renunciation and
love. And the religion of the weak taught *Down with the
strong and the powerful, and let the poor be glorified*. Since
there are always more weak people, than strong, in the
world, the second sort of Christianity has triumphed and

will triumph. If the weak are not ruled, they will rule, and
there's the end of it. And the rule of the weak is *Down with
the strong!*

The grand biblical authority for this cry is the Apocalypse. The weak and pseudo-humble are going to wipe all
worldly power, glory, and riches off the face of the earth,
and then they, the truly weak, are going to reign. It will
be a millennium of pseudo-humble saints, and gruesome to
contemplate. But it is what religion stands for today: down
with all strong, free life, let the weak triumph, let the
pseudo-humble reign. The religion of the self-glorification
of the weak, the reign of the pseudo-humble. This is the
spirit of society today, religious and political.

CHAPTER III

AND this was pretty well the religion of John of Patmos. They say he was an old man already when he finished the Apocalypse in the year A.D. 96: which is the date fixed by modern scholars, from 'internal evidence'.

Now there were three Johns in early Christian history: John the Baptist, who baptised Jesus, and who apparently founded a religion, or at least a sect of his own, with strange doctrines that continued for many years after Jesus's death; then there was the Apostle John, who was supposed to have written the Fourth Gospel and some Epistles; then there was this John of Patmos who lived in Ephesus and was sent to prison on Patmos for some religious offence against the Roman State. He was, however, released from his island after a term of years, returned to Ephesus, and lived, according to legend, to a great old age.

For a long time it was thought that the Apostle John, to whom we ascribe the Fourth Gospel, had written the Apocalypse also. But it cannot be that the same man wrote the two works, they are so alien to one another. The author of the Fourth Gospel was surely a cultured 'Greek' Jew, and one of the great inspirers of mystic, 'loving' Christianity. John of Patmos must have had a very different nature. He certainly has inspired very different feelings.

When we come to read it critically and seriously, we realise that the Apocalypse reveals a profoundly important Christian doctrine which has in it none of the real Christ, none of the real Gospel, none of the creative breath of Christianity, and is nevertheless perhaps the most effectual doctrine in the Bible. That is, it has had a greater effect on second-rate people throughout the Christian ages, than any other book in the Bible. The Apocalypse of John is, as it stands, the work of a second-rate mind. It appeals intensely to second-rate minds in every country and every century.

Strangely enough, unintelligible as it is, it has no doubt been the greatest source of inspiration to the vast mass of Christian minds—the vast mass being always second rate—since the first century, and we realise, to our horror, that this is what we are up against today; not Jesus nor Paul, but John of Patmos.

The Christian doctrine of love even at its best was an evasion. Even Jesus was going to reign 'hereafter', when his 'love' would be turned into confirmed power. This business of reigning in glory hereafter went to the root of Christianity, and is, of course, only an expression of frustrated desire to reign here and now. The Jews would not be put off: they were determined to reign on earth, so after the Temple of Jerusalem was smashed for the second time, about 200 B.C., they started in to imagine the coming of a Messiah militant and triumphant, who would conquer the world. The Christians took this up as the Second Advent of Christ, when Jesus was coming to give the gentile world its final whipping, and establish a rule of saints. John of Patmos extended this previously modest rule of saints (about forty years) to the grand round number of a thousand years, and so the Millennium took hold of the imagination of men.

And so there crept into the New Testament the grand Christian enemy, the power-spirit. At the very last moment, when the devil had been so beautifully shut out, in he slipped, dressed in apocalyptic disguise, and enthroned himself at the end of the book as Revelation.

For Revelation, be it said once and for all, is the revelation of the undying will-to-power in man, and its sanctification, its final triumph. If you have to suffer martyrdom, and if all the universe has to be destroyed in the process, still, still, still, O Christian, you shall reign as a king and set your foot on the necks of the old bosses!

This is the message of Revelation.

And just as inevitably as Jesus had to have a Judas Iscariot among his disciples, so did there have to be a Revelation in the New Testament.

Why? Because the nature of man demands it, and will always demand it.

The Christianity of Jesus applies to a part of our nature only. There is a big part to which it does not apply. And to this part, as the Salvation Army will show you, Revelation does apply.

The religions of renunciation, meditation, and self-knowledge are for individuals alone. But man is individual only in part of his nature. In another great part of him, he is collective.

The religions of renunciation, meditation, self-knowledge, pure morality are for individuals, and even then, not for complete individuals. But they express the individual side of man's nature. They isolate this side of his nature. And they cut off the other side of his nature, the collective side. The lowest stratum of society is always non-individual, so look there for the other manifestation of religion.

The religions of renunciation, like Buddhism or Christianity or Plato's philosophy, are for aristocrats, aristocrats of the spirit. The aristocrats of the spirit are to find their fulfilment in self-realisation and in service. Serve the poor. Well and good. But whom are the poor going to serve? It is a grand question. And John of Patmos answers it. The poor are going to serve themselves, and attend to their own self-glorification. And by the poor we don't mean the indigent merely; we mean the merely collective souls, terribly 'middling', who have no aristocratic singleness and aloneness.

The vast mass are these middling souls. They *have* no aristocratic individuality, such as is demanded by Christ or Buddha or Plato. So they skulk in a mass and secretly are bent on their own ultimate self-glorification. The Patmossers.

Only when he is alone, can man be a Christian, a Buddhist, or a Platonist. The Christ statues and Buddha statues witness to this. When he is with other men, instantly distinction occurs, and levels are formed. As soon as he is with other men, Jesus is an aristocrat, a master. Buddha is always the Lord Buddha. Francis of Assisi, trying to be so humble, as a matter of fact finds a subtle means to absolute power over his followers. Shelley could not *bear* to be the aristocrat of his company. Lenin was a Tyrannus in shabby clothes.

So it is! Power is there, and always will be. As soon as two or three men come together, especially to *do* something, then power comes into being, and one man is a leader, a master. It is inevitable.

Accept it, recognise the natural power in the man, as men did in the past, and give it homage, then there is a great joy, an uplifting, and a potency passes from the powerful to the less powerful. There is a stream of power. And in this, men have their best collective being, now and forever, and a corresponding flame springs up in yourself. Give homage and allegiance to a hero, and you become yourself heroic. It is the law of men. Perhaps the law of women is different.

But act on the reverse, and what happens! Deny power, and power wanes. Deny power in a greater man, and you have no power yourself. But society, now and forever, must be ruled and governed. So that the mass must grant *authority* where they deny power. Authority now takes the place of power, and we have 'ministers' and public officials and policemen. Then comes the grand scramble of ambition, competition, and the mass treading one another in the face, so afraid they are of power.

A man like Lenin is a great evil saint who believes in the utter destruction of power. It leaves men unutterably bare, stripped, mean, miserable, and humiliated. Abraham Lincoln is a half-evil saint who *almost* believes in the utter destruction of power. President Wilson is a quite evil saint who quite believes in the destruction of power—but who runs himself to megalomania and neurasthenic tyranny. Every saint becomes evil—and Lenin, Lincoln, Wilson are true saints so long as they remain purely individual;—every saint becomes evil the moment he touches the collective self of men. Then he is a perverter: Plato the same. The great saints are for the *individual* only, and that means, for one side of our nature only, for in the deep layers of ourselves we are collective, we can't help it. And the collective self either lives and moves and has its being in a full relationship of power: or it is reserved, and lives a frictional misery of trying to destroy power, and destroy itself.

But nowadays, the will to destroy power is paramount. Great kings like the Tzar—we mean great in position—are rendered almost imbecile by the vast anti-will of the masses, the will to negate power. Modern kings are negated till they become almost idiots. And the same of any man in power, unless he be a power-destroyer and a white-feathered evil bird: then the mass will back him up. How can the anti-power masses, above all the great middling

masses, ever have a king who is more than a thing of ridi-
cule or pathos?

The Apocalypse has been running for nearly two thousand years: the hidden side of Christianity: and its work
is nearly done. For the Apocalypse does not worship power.
It wants to murder the powerful, to seize the power itself,
the weakling.

Judas had to betray Jesus to the powers that be, because
of the denial and subterfuge inherent in Jesus's teaching.
Jesus took up the position of the pure individual, even with
his disciples. He did not *really* mix with them, or even
really work or act with them. *He was alone all the time.* He
puzzled them utterly, and in some part of them, he let them
down. He refused to be their physical power-lord: the
power-homage in a man like Judas felt itself betrayed! So
it betrayed back again: with a kiss. And in the same way,
Revelation had to be included in the New Testament, to
give the death kiss to the Gospels.

CHAPTER IV

IT is a curious thing, but the collective will of a community really reveals the *basis* of the individual will. The early Christian Churches, or communities, revealed quite early a strange will to a strange kind of power. They had a will to destroy all power, and so usurp themselves the final, the ultimate power. This was not quite the teaching of Jesus, but it was the inevitable implication of Jesus's teaching, in the minds of the vast mass of the weak, the inferior. Jesus taught the escape and liberation into unselfish, brotherly love: a feeling that only the strong can know. And this, sure enough, at once brought the community of the weak into triumphant being; and the will of the community of Christians was anti-social, almost anti-human, revealing from the start a frenzied desire for the end of the world, the destruction of humanity altogether; and then, when this did not come, a grim determination to destroy all mastery, all lordship, and all human splendour out of the world, leaving only the community of saints as the final negation of power, and the final power.

After the crash of the Dark Ages, the Catholic Church emerged again a *human* thing, a complete, not a half-thing, adjusted to seed-time and harvest and the solstice of Christmas and of mid-summer, and having a good balance, in early days, between brotherly love and natural lordship and splendour. Every man was given his little kingdom in marriage, and every woman her own little inviolate realm. This Christian marriage guided by the Church was a great institution for true freedom, true possibility of fulfilment. Freedom was no more, and can be no more than the possibility of living fully and satisfactorily. In marriage, in the great natural cycle of church ritual and festival, the early Catholic Church tried to give this to men. But alas, the Church soon fell out of balance, into worldly greed.

18 APOCALYPSE

Then came the Reformation, and the thing started over again: the old will of the Christian community to destroy human worldly power, and to substitute the *negative* power of the mass. The battle rages today, in all its horror. In Russia, the triumph over worldly power was accomplished, and the reign of saints set in, with Lenin for the chief saint.

And Lenin was a saint. He had every quality of a saint. He is worshipped today, quite rightly, as a saint. But saints who try to kill all brave power in mankind are fiends, like the Puritans who wanted to pull all the bright feathers out of the chaffinch. Fiends!

Lenin's rule of saints turned out quite horrible. It has more thou-shalt-nots than any rule of 'Beasts', or emperors. And this is bound to be so. Any rule of saints must be horrible. Why? Because the nature of man is not saintly. The *primal* need, the old-Adamic need in a man's soul is to be, in his own sphere and as far as he can attain it, master, lord, and splendid one. Every cock can crow on his own muck-heap, and ruffle gleaming feathers; every peasant could be a glorious little Tzar in his own hut, and when he got a bit drunk. And every peasant was consummated in the old dash and gorgeousness of the nobles, and in the supreme splendour of the Tzar. The supreme master and lord and splendid one: their own, their own splendid one: they might see him with their own eyes, the Tzar! And this fulfilled one of the deepest, greatest, and most powerful needs of the human heart. The human heart needs, needs, needs, splendour, gorgeousness, pride, assumption, glory, and lordship. Perhaps it needs these even more than it needs love: at least, even more than bread. And every great king makes every man a little lord in his own tiny sphere, fills the imagination with lordship and splendour, satisfies the soul. The most dangerous thing in the world is to show man his own paltriness as hedged-in male. It depresses him, and *makes* him paltry. We become, alas, what we think we are. Men have been depressed now for many years in their male and splendid selves, depressed into dejection and almost into abjection. Is not that evil? Then let men themselves do something about it.

And a great saint like Lenin—or Shelley or St. Francis—can only cry *anathema! anathema!* to the natural proud self of power, and try deliberately to destroy all might and all lordship, and leave the people poor, oh, so poor! Poor, poor, poor, as the people are in all our modern democracies, though nowhere so absolutely impoverished in life as in the most absolute democracy, no matter how they be in money.

The community is inhuman, and less than human. It becomes at last the most dangerous because *bloodless* and insentient tyrant. For a long time, even a democracy like the American or the Swiss will answer to the call of a hero, who is somewhat of a true aristocrat: like Lincoln: so strong is the aristocratic instinct in man. But the willingness to give the response to the heroic, the true aristocratic call, gets weaker and weaker in every democracy, as time goes on. All history proves it. Then men turn against the heroic appeal, with a sort of venom. They will only listen to the call of mediocrity wielding the insentient bullying power of mediocrity: which is evil. Hence the success of painfully inferior and even base politicians.

Brave people add up to an aristocracy. The democracy of thou-shalt-not is bound to be a collection of weak men. And then the sacred 'will of the people' becomes blinder, baser, and more dangerous than the will of any tyrant. When the will of the people becomes the sum of the weakness of a multitude of weak men, it is time to make a break.

So today. Society consists of a mass of weak individuals trying to protect themselves, out of fear, from every possible imaginary evil, and, of course, *by their very fear*, bringing the evil into being.

This is the Christian community today, in its perpetual mean thou-shalt-not. This is how Christian doctrine has worked out in practice.

CHAPTER V

AND Revelation was a foreshadowing of all this. It is above all what some psychologists would call the revelation of a thwarted 'superiority' goal, and a consequent inferiority complex. Of the positive side of Christianity, the peace of meditation and the joy of unselfish service, the rest from ambition and the pleasure of knowledge, we find nothing in the Apocalypse. Because the Apocalypse is for the non-individual side of a man's nature, written from the thwarted collective self, whereas meditation and unselfish service are for pure individuals, isolate. Pure Christianity anyhow *cannot* fit a nation, or society at large. The great war made it obvious. It can only fit individuals. The collective whole must have some other inspiration.

And the Apocalypse, repellent though its chief spirit be, does also contain another inspiration. It is repellent because it resounds with the dangerous snarl of the *frustrated, suppressed* collective self, the frustrated power-spirit in man, vengeful. But it contains also some revelation of the true and positive power-spirit. The very beginning surprises us: 'John to the seven churches in Asia: grace be to you and peace from HE WHO IS AND WAS AND IS COMING, and from the seven Spirits before his throne, and from Jesus Christ the faithful witness, the first-born from the dead, and the prince over the kings of the earth; to him who loves us and loosed us from our sins by shedding his blood—he has made us a realm of priests for his God and Father—to him be glory and dominion for ever and ever, Amen. Lo, he is coming on the clouds, to be seen by every eye, even by those who impaled him, and all the tribes of earth will wail because of him: even so, Amen.'—I have used Moffatt's translation, as the meaning is a little more explicit than in the authorised version.

But here we have a curious Jesus, very different from

the one in Galilee, wandering by the lake. And the book
goes on: 'On the Lord's day I found myself rapt in the Spirit,
and I heard a loud voice behind me like a trumpet calling,
"Write your vision in a book."—So I turned to see whose
voice it was that spoke to me; and on turning round I saw
seven golden lampstands and in the middle of the lampstands One who resembled a human being, with a long robe,
and a belt of gold round his breast; his head and hair were
white as wool, white as snow; his eyes flashed like fire, his
feet glowed like burnished bronze, his voice sounded like
many waves, in his right hand he held seven stars, a sharp
sword with a double edge issued from his mouth, and his
face shone like the sun in full strength. When I saw him, I
fell at his feet like a dead man; but he laid his hand on me,
saying: 'Do not be afraid; I am the First and Last, I was
dead and here I am alive for evermore, holding the keys
that unlock death and Hades. Write down your vision of
what is and what is to be hereafter. As for the secret symbol
of the seven stars which you have seen in my right hand,
and of the seven golden lampstands: the seven stars are the
angels of the seven churches, and the seven lampstands are
the seven churches. To the angel of the church at Ephesus
write thus:— 'These are the words of him who holds the
seven stars in his right hand, who moves among the seven
golden lampstands——' " '

Now this being with the sword of the Logos issuing from
his mouth and the seven stars in his hand is the Son of God,
therefore, the Messiah, therefore Jesus. It is very far from
the Jesus who said in Gethsemane: 'My heart is sad, sad
even unto death; stay here and watch.'—But it is the Jesus
that the early Church, especially in Asia, prominently believed in.

And what is this Jesus? It is the great Splendid One,
almost identical with the Almighty in the visions of Ezekiel
and Daniel. It is a vast cosmic lord, standing among the
seven eternal lamps of the archaic planets, sun and moon
and five great stars around his feet. In the sky his gleaming
head is in the north, the sacred region of the Pole, and he
holds in his right hand the seven stars of the Bear, that we
call the Plough, and he wheels them round the Pole star, as
even now we see them wheel, causing universal revolution
of the heavens, the roundwise moving of the cosmos. This

is the lord of all motion, who swings the cosmos into its course. Again, from his mouth issues the two-edged sword of the Word, the mighty weapon of the Logos which will smite the world (and in the end destroy it). This is the sword indeed that Jesus brought among men. And lastly, his face shines like the sun in full strength, the source of life itself, the dazzler, before whom we fall as if dead.

And this is Jesus: not only the Jesus of the early churches, but the Jesus of popular religion today. There is nothing humble nor suffering here. It is our 'superiority goal', indeed. And it is a true account of man's *other* conception of God; perhaps the greater and more fundamental conception: the magnificent Mover of the Cosmos! To John of Patmos, the Lord is *Kosmokrator*, and even *Kosmodynamos*; the great Ruler of the Cosmos, and the Power of the Cosmos. But alas, according to the Apocalypse man has no share in the ruling of the cosmos until after death. When a Christian has been put to death by martyrdom, then he will be resurrected at the Second Advent and become himself a little Kosmokrator, ruling for a thousand years. It is the apotheosis of the weak man.

But the Son of God, the Jesus of John's vision, is more even than this. He holds the keys that unlock death and Hades. He is Lord of the Underworld. He is Hermes, the guide of souls through the death-world, over the hellish stream. He is master of the mysteries of the dead, he knows the meaning of the holocaust, and has final power over the powers below. The dead and the lords of death, who are always hovering in the background of religion away down among the people, these chthonioi of the primitive Greeks, these too must acknowledge Jesus as a supreme lord.

And the lord of the dead is master of the future, and the god of the present. He gives the vision of what was, and is, and shall be.

Here is a Jesus for you! What is modern Christianity going to make of it? For it is the Jesus of the very first communities, and it is the Jesus of the early Catholic Church, as it emerged from the Dark Ages and adjusted itself once more to life and death and the cosmos, the whole great adventure of the human soul, as contrasted with the little petty personal adventure of modern Protestantism and Catholicism alike, cut off from the cosmos, cut off from

Hades, cut off from the magnificence of the Star-mover. Petty little personal salvation, petty morality instead of cosmic splendour, we have lost the sun and the planets, and the Lord with the seven stars of the Bear in his right hand. Poor, paltry, creeping little world we live in, even the keys of death and Hades are lost. How shut in we are! All we can do, with our brotherly love, is to shut one another in. We are so afraid somebody else might be lordly and splendid, when we can't. Petty little bolshevists, every one of us today, we are determined that *no* man shall shine like the sun in full strength, for he would certainly outshine us.

Now again we realise a dual feeling in ourselves with regard to the Apocalypse. Suddenly we see some of the old pagan splendour, that delighted in the might and the magnificence of the cosmos, and man who was as a star in the cosmos. Suddenly we feel again the nostalgia for the old pagan world, long before John's day, we feel an immense yearning to be freed from this petty personal entanglement of weak life, to be back in the far-off world before men became 'afraid'. We want to be freed from our tight little automatic 'universe', to go back to the great living cosmos of the 'unenlightened' pagans.

Perhaps the greatest difference between us and the pagans lies in our different relation to the cosmos. With us, all is personal. Landscape and the sky, these are to us the delicious background of our personal life, and no more. Even the universe of the scientist is little more than an extension of our personality, to us. To the pagan, landscape and personal background were on the whole indifferent. But the cosmos was a very real thing. A man *lived* with the cosmos, and knew it greater than himself.

Don't let us imagine we see the sun as the old civilisations saw it. All we see is a scientific little luminary, dwindled to a ball of blazing gas. In the centuries before Ezekiel and John, the sun was still a magnificent reality, men drew forth from him strength and splendour, and gave him back homage and lustre and thanks. But in us, the connection is broken, the responsive centres are dead. Our sun is a quite different thing from the cosmic sun of the ancients, so much more trivial. We may see what we call the sun, but we have lost Helios forever, and the great orb of the Chaldeans still more. We have lost the cosmos, by coming out of responsive connection with it, and this is our chief tragedy. What is our petty little love of nature—Nature!! —compared to the ancient magnificent living with the cosmos, and being honoured by the cosmos!

And some of the great images of the Apocalypse move us to strange depths, and to a strange wild fluttering of freedom : of true freedom, really, an escape to somewhere, not an escape to nowhere. An escape from the tight little cage of our universe; tight, in spite of all the astronomist's vast and unthinkable stretches of space; tight, because it is only a continuous extension, a dreary on and on, without any meaning : an escape from this into the vital cosmos, to a sun who has a great wild life, and who looks back at us for strength or withering, marvellous, as he goes his way. Who says the sun cannot speak to me! The sun has a great blazing consciousness, and I have a little blazing consciousness. When I can strip myself of the trash of personal feelings and ideas, and get down to my naked sun-self, then the sun and I can commune by the hour, the blazing interchange, and he gives me life, sun-life, and I send him a little new brightness from the world of the bright blood. The great sun, like an angry dragon, hater of the nervous and personal consciousness in us. As all these modern sunbathers must realise, for they become disintegrated by the very sun that bronzes them. But the sun, like a lion, loves the bright red blood of life, and can give it an infinite enrichment if we know how to receive it. But we don't. We have lost the sun. And he only falls on us and destroys us, decomposing something in us : the dragon of destruction instead of the life-bringer.

And we have lost the moon, the cool, bright, ever-varying moon. It is she who would caress our nerves, smooth them with the silky hand of her glowing, soothe them into serenity again with her cool presence. For the moon is the mistress and mother of our watery bodies, the pale body of our nervous consciousness and our moist flesh. Oh, the moon could soothe us and heal us like a cool great Artemis between her arms. But we have lost her, in our stupidity we ignore her, and angry she stares down on us and whips us with nervous whips. Oh, beware of the angry Artemis of the night heavens, beware of the spite of Cybele, beware of the vindictiveness of horned Astarte.

For the lovers who shoot themselves in the night, in the horrible suicide of love, they are driven mad by the poisoned arrows of Artemis: the moon is against them: the moon is fiercely against them. And oh, if the moon is against you, oh, beware of the bitter night, especially the night of intoxication.

Now this may sound nonsense, but that is merely because we are fools. There is an eternal vital correspondence between our blood and the sun: there is an eternal vital correspondence between our nerves and the moon. If we get out of contact and harmony with the sun and moon, then both turn into great dragons of destruction against us. The sun is a great source of blood-vitality, it streams strength to us. But once we resist the sun, and say: It is a mere ball of gas!—then the very streaming vitality of sunshine turns into subtle disintegrative force in us, and undoes us. The same with the moon, the planets, the great stars. They are either our makers or our unmakers. There is no escape.

We and the cosmos are one. The cosmos is a vast living body, of which we are still parts. The sun is a great heart whose tremors run through our smallest veins. The moon is a great gleaming nerve-centre from which we quiver forever. Who knows the power that Saturn has over us, or Venus? But it is a vital power, rippling exquisitely through us *all the time*. And if we deny Aldebaran, Aldebaran will pierce us with infinite dagger-thrusts. He who is not with me!—that is a cosmic law.

Now all this is *literally* true, as men knew in the great past, and as they will know again.

By the time of John of Patmos, men, especially educated men, had already almost lost the cosmos. The sun, the moon, the planets, instead of being the communers, the comminglers, the life-givers, the splendid ones, the awful ones, had already fallen into a sort of deadness; they were the arbitrary, almost mechanical engineers of fate and destiny. By the time of Jesus, men had turned the heavens into a mechanism of fate and destiny, a prison. The Christians escaped this prison by denying the body altogether. But alas, these little escapes! especially the escapes by denial! —they are the most fatal of evasions. Christianity and our ideal civilisation have been one long evasion. It has caused endless lying and misery, misery such as people know today, not of physical want but of far more deadly vital want. Better lack bread than lack life. The long evasion, whose only fruit is the machine!

We have lost the cosmos. The sun strengthens us no more, neither does the moon. In mystic language, the moon is black to us, and the sun is as sackcloth.

Now we have to get back the cosmos, and it can't be done by a trick. The great range of responses that have fallen dead in us have to come to life again. It has taken two thousand years to kill them. Who knows how long it will take to bring them to life?

When I hear modern people complain of being lonely then I know what has happened. They have lost the cosmos. —It is nothing human and personal that we are short of. What we lack is cosmic life, the sun in us and the moon in us. We can't get the sun in us by lying naked like pigs on a beach. The very sun that is bronzing us is inwardly disintegrating us—as we know later. Process of katabolism. We can only get the sun by a sort of worship: and the same with the moon. By *going forth* to worship the sun, worship that is felt in the blood. Tricks and postures only make matters worse.

CHAPTER VI

AND now we must admit that we are also grateful to St. John's Revelation for giving us hints of the magnificent cosmos and putting us into momentary contact. The contacts, it is true, are only for moments, then they are broken by this other spirit of hope-despair. But even for the moments we are grateful.

There are flashes throughout the first part of the Apocalypse of true cosmic worship. The cosmos became anathema to the Christians, though the early Catholic Church restored it somewhat after the crash of the Dark Ages. Then again the cosmos became anathema to the Protestants after the Reformation. They substituted the non-vital universe of forces and mechanistic order, everything else became abstraction, and the long, slow death of the human being set in. This slow death produced science and machinery, but both are death products.

No doubt the death was necessary. It is the long, slow death of society which parallels the quick death of Jesus and the other dying gods. It is death none the less, and will end in the annihilation of the human race—as John of Patmos so fervently hoped—unless there is a change, a resurrection, and a return to the cosmos.

But these flashes of the cosmos in Revelation can hardly be attributed to John of Patmos. As apocalyptist he uses other people's flashes to light up his way of woe and hope. The grand hope of the Christians is a measure of their utter despair.

It began, however, before the Christians. Apocalypse is a curious form of literature, Jewish and Jewish-Christian. This new form arose somewhere about 200 B.C., when the prophets had finished. An early Apocalypse is the Book of Daniel, the latter part at least: another is the Apocalypse of Enoch, the oldest parts of which are attributed to the second century B.C.

The Jews, the Chosen People, had always had an idea of themselves as a grand imperial people. They had their try, and failed disastrously. Then they gave it up. After the destruction they ceased to imagine a great natural Jewish Empire. The prophets became silent forever. The Jews became a people of *postponed destiny*. And then the seers began to write Apocalypses.

The seers had to tackle this business of postponed destiny. It was no longer a matter of prophecy: it was a matter of vision. God would no longer *tell* his servant what would happen, for what would happen was almost untellable. He would show him a vision.

Every profound new movement makes a great swing also backwards to some older, half-forgotten way of consciousness. So the apocalyptists swung back to the old cosmic vision. After the second destruction of the Temple of the Jews despaired, consciously or unconsciously, of the *earthly* triumph of the Chosen People. Therefore, doggedly, they prepared for an unearthly triumph. That was what the apocalyptists set out to do: to vision forth the unearthly triumph of the Chosen.

To do this, they needed an all-round view: they needed to know the end as well as the beginning. Never before had men wanted to know the end of creation: sufficient that it was created, and would go on for ever and ever. But now, the apocalyptists had to have a vision of the end.

They became then cosmic. Enoch's visions of the cosmos are very interesting, and not very Jewish. But they are curiously geographical.

When we come to John's Apocalypse, and come to know it, several things strike us. First, the obvious scheme, the division of the book into two halves, with two rather discordant intentions. The first half, before the birth of the baby Messiah, seems to have the intention of salvation and renewal, leaving the world to go on renewed. But the second half, when the Beasts rouse up, develops a weird and mystic hate of the world, of worldly power, and of everything and everybody who does not submit to the Messiah out and out. The second half of the Apocalypse is flamboyant hate and simple lust, lust is the only word, for the end of the world. The apocalyptist *must* see the universe, or the known cosmos, wiped out utterly, and merely a heavenly city and a hellish lake of brimstone left.

The discrepancy of the two intentions is the first thing that strikes us. The first part, briefer, more condensed or abbreviated, is much more difficult and complicated than the second part, and the feeling in it is much more dramatic, yet more universal and significant. We feel in the first part, we know not why, the space and pageantry of the pagan world. In the second part is the individual frenzy of those early Christians, rather like the frenzies of chapel people and revivalists today.

Then again, we feel that in the first part we are in touch with great old symbols, that take us far back into time, into the pagan vistas. In the second part, the imagery is Jewish allegorical, rather modern, and has a fairly easy local and temporal explanation. When there is a touch of true symbolism, it is not of the nature of a ruin or a remains embedded in the present structure, it is rather an archaic reminiscence.

A third thing that strikes us is the persistent use of the great pagan, as well as Jewish power-titles, both for God and for the Son of Man. *King of Kings and Lord of Lords* is typical throughout, and Kosmokrator, and Kosmodynamos. Always the titles of power, and never the titles of love. Always Christ the omnipotent conqueror flashing his great sword and destroying, destroying vast masses of men, till blood mounts up to the horses' bridles. Never Christ the Saviour: never. The Son of Man of the Apocalypse comes to bring a new and terrible *power* on to the earth, greater than that of any Pompey or Alexander or Cyrus. Power, terrific, smiting power. And when praise is uttered, or the hymn to the Son of Man, it is to ascribe to him power, and riches, and wisdom, and strength, and honour, and glory, and blessing—all the attributes given to the great kings and Pharaohs of the earth, but hardly suited to a crucified Jesus.

So that we are left puzzled. If John of Patmos finished this Apocalypse in A.D. 96, he knew strangely little of the Jesus legend, and had just none of the spirit of the Gospels, all of which preceded his book. A curious being, this old John of Patmos, whoever he was. But anyhow he focussed the emotions of certain types of men for centuries to come.

What we feel about the Apocalypse is that it is not one book but several, perhaps many. But it is not made up of pieces of several books strung together, like Enoch. It is one book, in several layers: like layers of civilization as you dig deeper and deeper to excavate an old city. Down at the bottom is a pagan substratum, probably one of the ancient books of the Aegean civilisation: some sort of book of a pagan Mystery. This has been written over by Jewish apocalyptists, then extended, and then finally written over by the Jewish-Christian apocalyptist John: and then, after his day, expurgated and corrected and pruned down and added to by Christian editors who wanted to make of it a Christian work.

But John of Patmos must have been a strange Jew: violent, full of the Hebrew books of the Old Testament, but also full of all kinds of pagan knowledge, anything that would contribute to his passion, his unbearable passion, for the Second Advent, the utter smiting of the Romans with the great sword of Christ, the trampling of mankind in the winepress of God's anger till blood mounted to the bridles of the horses, the triumph of the rider on a white horse, greater than any Persian king: then the rule of martyrs for one thousand years: and then, oh then the destruction of the entire universe, and the last Judgment. 'Come, Lord Jesus, Come!'

And John firmly believed he was coming, and coming *immediately*. Therein lay the trembling of the terrific and terrifying hope of the early Christians: that made them, naturally, in pagan eyes, the enemies of mankind altogether.

But He did not come, so we are not very much interested. What does interest us is the strange pagan recoil of the book, and the pagan vestiges. And we realise how the Jew, when he *does* look into the outside world, has to look with pagan or gentile eyes. The Jews of the post-David period had no eyes of their own to see with. They peered inward at their Jehovah till they were blind: then they looked at the world with the eyes of their neighbours. When the prophets had to see visions, they had to see Assyrian or Chaldean visions. They borrowed other gods to see their own invisible God by.

Ezekiel's great vision, which is so largely repeated in the Apocalypse, what is it but pagan, disfigured probably by jealous Jewish scribes? a great pagan concept of the Time Spirit and the Kosmokrator and the Kosmodynamos! Add to this that the Kosmokrator stands among the wheels of the heavens, known as the wheels of Anaximander, and we see where we are. We are in the great world of the pagan cosmos.

But the text of Ezekiel is hopelessly corrupt—no doubt deliberately corrupted by fanatical scribes who wanted to smear over the pagan vision. It is an old story.

It is none the less amazing to find Anaximander's wheels in Ezekiel. These wheels are an ancient attempt to explain the orderly yet complex movement of the heavens. They are based on the first 'scientific' duality which the pagans found in the universe, namely, the moist and the dry, the cold and the hot, air (or cloud) and fire. Strange and fascinating are the great revolving wheels of the sky, made of dense air or night-cloud and filled with the blazing cosmic fire, which fire peeps through or blazes through at certain holes in the felloes of the wheels, and forms the blazing sun or the pointed stars. All the orbs are little holes in the black wheel which is full of fire: and there is wheel within wheel, revolving differently.

Anaximander, almost the very first of the ancient Greek thinkers, is supposed to have invented this 'wheel' theory of the heavens in Ionia in the sixth century B.C. Anyhow Ezekiel learnt it in Babylonia: and who knows whether the whole idea is not Chaldean. Surely it has behind it centuries of Chaldean sky-knowledge.

It is a great relief to find Anaximander's wheels in Ezekiel. The Bible at once becomes a book of the human race, instead of a corked-up bottle of 'inspiration'. And so it is a relief to find the four Creatures of the four quarters of the heavens, winged and starry. Immediately we are out in the great Chaldean star-spaces, instead of being pinched up in a Jewish tabernacle. That the Jews managed, by pernicious anthropomorphising, to turn the four great Creatures into Archangels, even with names like Michael and Gabriel, only shows the limit of the Jewish imagination, which can know nothing except in terms of the human ego. It is none the less a relief to know that these policemen of God, the great Archangels, were once the winged and starry creatures of the four quarters of the heavens, quivering their wings across space, in Chaldean lore.

In John of Patmos, the 'wheels' are missing. They had been superseded long ago by the spheres of the heavens. But the Almighty is even more distinctly a cosmic wonder, amber-coloured like sky-fire, the great Maker and the great Ruler of the starry heavens, Demiurge and Kosmokrator, the one who wheels the cosmos. He is a great *actual* figure, the great dynamic god, neither spiritual nor moral, but cosmic and vital.

Naturally or unnaturally, the orthodox critics deny this. Archdeacon Charles admits that the seven stars in the right hand of the 'Son of Man' are the stars of the Bear, wheeling round the Pole, and that this is Babylonian: then he goes on to say 'but our author can have had nothing of this in mind.'

Of course, excellent clergymen of today know exactly what 'our author' had in mind. John of Patmos is a Christian saint, so he *couldn't* have had any heathenism in mind. This is what orthodox criticism amounts to. Whereas as a matter of fact we are amazed at the almost brutal paganism of 'our author', John of Patmos. Whatever else he was, he was not afraid of a pagan symbol, nor even, apparently, of a whole pagan cult. The old religions were cults of vitality, potency, and power: we must never forget it. Only the Hebrews were moral: and they only in patches. Among the old pagans, morals were just social manners, decent behaviour. But by the time of Christ all religion and all thought seemed to turn from the old worship and study of vitality, potency, power, to the study of death and death-rewards, death-penalties, and morals. All religion, instead of being religion of *life*, here and now, became religion of postponed destiny, death, and reward *afterwards*, 'if you are good'.

John of Patmos accepted the postponement of destiny with a vengeance, but he cared little about 'being good'. What he wanted was the *ultimate* power. He was a shameless, power-worshipping pagan Jew, gnashing his teeth over the postponement of his grand destiny.

It seems to me he knew a good deal about the pagan value of symbols, as contrasted even with the Jewish or Christian value. And he used the pagan value just when it suited him, for he was no timid soul. To suggest that the figure of the Kosmodynamos wheeling the heavens, the great figure of cosmic Fire with the seven stars of the Bear in his right hand, could be unknown to John of Patmos is beyond even an archdeacon. The world of the first century was full of star-cults, the figure of the Mover of the Heavens must have been familiar to every boy in the east. Orthodox critics in one breath relate that 'our author' had no starry heathenism in mind, and in the next they expatiate on how thankful men must have been to escape, through Christianity, from the senseless and mechanical domination of the heavens, the changeless rule of the planets, the fixed astronomical and astrological fate. 'Good heavens!' we still exclaim: and if we pause to consider, we shall see how powerful was the idea of moving, fate-fixing heavens, half cosmic, half mechanical, but still not anthropomorphic.

I am sure not only John of Patmos, but St. Paul and St. Peter and St. John the Apostle knew a great deal about the stars, and about the pagan cults. They chose, perhaps wisely, to suppress it all. John of Patmos did not. So his Christian critics and editors, from the second century down to Archdeacon Charles, have tried to suppress it for him. Without success: because the kind of mind that worships the divine *power* always tends to think in symbols. Direct thinking in symbols, like a game of chess, with its king and queen and pawns, is characteristic of those men who see power as the great desideratum—and they are the majority. The lowest substratum of the people still worships power, still thinks crudely in symbols, still sticks to the Apocalypse and is entirely callous to the Sermon on the Mount. But so, apparently, does the highest superstratum of church and state still worship in terms of power: naturally, really.

But the orthodox critics like Archdeacon Charles want to have their cake and eat it. They *want* the old pagan power-sense in the Apocalypse, and they spend half their time denying it is there. If they *have* to admit a pagan element, they gather up the skirts of their clerical gowns and hurry past. And at the same time, the Apocalypse is a veritable heathen feast for them. Only they must swallow it with pious appearances.

Of course the dishonesty, we can call it no less, of the Christian critic is based on fear. Once start admitting that *anything* in the Bible is pagan, of pagan origin and meaning,

and you are lost, you won't know where to stop. God escapes
out of the bottle once and for all, to put it irreverently.
The Bible is so splendidly full of paganisms and therein lies
its greater interest. But once admit it, and Christianity must
come out of her shell.

Once more then we look at the Apocalypse, and try to
sense its structure vertically, as well as horizontally. For
the more we read it, the more we feel that it is a section
through time, as well as a Messianic mystery. It is the
work of no one man, and even of no one century, of that
we feel sure.

The oldest part, surely, was a pagan work, probably the
description of the 'secret' ritual of initiation into one of
the pagan Mysteries, Artemis, Cybele, even Orphic: but
most probably belonging there to the east Mediterranean,
probably actually to Ephesus: as would seem natural. If
such a book existed, say two or perhaps three centuries
before Christ, then it was known to all students of religion:
and perhaps it would be safe to say that every intelligent
man in that day, especially in the east, was a student of
religion. Men were religious-mad: not religious-sane. The
Jews were just the same as the gentiles. The Jews of the
dispersion certainly read and discussed everything they
could lay their hands on. We must put away forever the
Sunday-school idea of a bottled-up Jewry with nothing but
its own god to think about. It was very different. The Jews
of the last centuries B.C. were as curious, as widely read,
and as cosmopolitan as the Jews of today: saving, of course,
a few fanatical sets and sects.

So that the old pagan book must quite early have been
taken and written over by a Jewish apocalyptist, with a
view to substituting the Jewish idea of a Messiah and a
Jewish salvation (or destruction) of the whole world, for
the purely individual experience of pagan initiation. This
Jewish Apocalypse, written over perhaps more than once,
was surely known to all religious seekers of Jesus's day, including the writers of the Gospel. And probably, even before
John of Patmos tackled it, a Jewish-Christian apocalyptist
had rewritten the work once more, probably had already
extended it in the prophetic manner of Daniel, to foretell
the utter downfall of Rome: for the Jews loved nothing
in the world so much as prophesying the utter downfall of

the gentile kingdoms. Then John of Patmos occupied his prison-years on the island in writing the whole book over once more, in his own peculiar style. We feel that he invented little, and had few ideas: but that he did indeed have a fierce and burning passion against the Romans who had condemned him. For all that, he shows no hatred of the pagan Greek culture of the east. In fact, he accepts it almost as naturally as his own Hebrew culture, and far more naturally than the new Christian spirit, which is alien to him. He rewrites the older Apocalypse, probably cuts the pagan passages still shorter, simply because they have no Messianic anti-Rome purport, not for any objection to their paganism; and then he lets himself go in the second half of the book, where he can lash the Beast called Rome (or Babylon), the Beast called Nero, or Nero redivivus, and the Beast called Antichrist, or the Roman priesthood of the Imperial cult. How he left the final chapters about the New Jerusalem we don't know, but they are now in a state of confusion.

We feel that John was a violent but not very profound person. If he invented the letters to the seven churches, they are a rather dull and weak contribution. And yet it is his curious fervid intensity which gives to Revelation its lurid power. And we cannot help liking him for leaving the great symbols on the whole intact.

But after John had done with it, the real Christians started in. And that we really resent. The Christian fear of the pagan outlook has damaged the whole consciousness of man. The one fixed attitude of Christianity towards the pagan religious vision has been an attitude of stupid denial, denial that there was anything in the pagans at all, except bestiality. And all pagan evidence in the books of the Bible had to be expurgated, or twisted into meaninglessness, or smeared over into Christian or Jewish semblances.

This is what happened to the Apocalypse after John left it. How many bits the little Christian scribes have snipped out, how many bits they have stuck in, how many times they have forged 'our author's' style, we shall never know: but there are certainly many evidences of their pettifogging work. And all to cover up the pagan traces, and make this plainly unchristian work passably Christian.

We cannot help hating the Christian *fear*, whose method,

from the very beginning, has been to deny everything that didn't fit: or better still, suppress it. The system of suppression of all pagan evidence has been instinctive, a fearinstinct, and has been thorough, and has been really criminal, in the Christian world, from the first century until today. When a man thinks of the vast stores of priceless pagan documents that the Christians have wilfully destroyed, from the time of Nero to the obscure parish priests of today, who still burn any book found in their parish that is unintelligible, and therefore possibly heretical, the mind stands still!—and we reflect with irony on the hullabaloo over Rheims Cathedral. How many of the books we would give our fingers to possess, and can't, are lost because the Christians burnt them on purpose! They left Plato and Aristotle, feeling these two kin. But the others—!

The instinctive policy of Christianity towards all true pagan evidence has been and is still—suppress it, destroy it, deny it. This dishonesty has vitiated Christian thought from the start. It has, even more curiously, vitiated ethnological scientific thought the same. Curiously enough, we do not look on the Greeks and the Romans, after about 600 B.C., as *real* pagans: not like Hindus or Persians, Babylonians or Egyptians, or even Cretans, for example. We accept the Greeks and Romans as the initiators of our intellectual and political civilisation, the Jews as the fathers of our moralreligious civilisation. So these are 'our sort'. All the rest are mere nothing, almost idiots. All that can be attributed to the 'barbarian' beyond the Greek pale: that is, to Minoans, Etruscans, Egyptians, Chaldeans, Persians, and Hindus, is, in the famous phrase of a famous German professor: *Urdummheit*. Urdummheit, or primal stupidity, is the state of all mankind before precious Homer, and of all races, all, except Greek, Jew, Roman, and—ourselves!

The strange thing is that even true scholars, who write scholarly and impartial books about the early Greeks, as soon as they mention the autochthonous races of the Mediterranean, or the Egyptians, or the Chaldeans, insist on the childishness of these peoples, their perfectly trivial achievement, their necessary Urdummheit. These great civilised peoples knew nothing: all *true* knowledge started with Thales and Anaximander and Pythagoras, with the Greeks. The Chaldeans knew no true astronomy, the Egyptians knew no mathematics or science, and the poor Hindus, who for centuries were supposed to have invented that highly important reality, the arithmetical zero, or nought, are now not allowed even this merit. The Arabs, who are almost 'us', invented it.

It is most strange. We can understand the *Christian* fear of the pagan way of knowledge. But why the scientific fear? Why should science betray its fear in a phrase like Urdummheit? We look at the wonderful remains of Egypt, Babylon, Assyria, Persia, and old India, and we repeat to ourselves: *Urdummheit!* Urdummheit? We look at the Etruscan tombs and ask ourselves again, *Urdummheit?* primal stupidity! Why, in the oldest of peoples, in the Egyptian friezes and the Assyrian, in the Etruscan paintings and the Hindu carvings we see a splendour, a beauty, and very often a joyous, sensitive intelligence which is certainly lost in our world of Neufrechheit. If it is a question of primal stupidity or new impudence, then give me primal stupidity.

The Archdeacon Charles is a true scholar and authority in Apocalypse, a far-reaching student of his subject. He tries, without success, to be fair in the matter of pagan origins. His predisposition, his terrific prejudice, is too strong for him. And once, he gives himself away, so we understand the whole process. He is writing in time of war—at the end of the late war—so we must allow for the fever. But he makes a bad break, none the less. On page 86 of the second volume of his commentary on Revelation, he writes of the Antichrist in the Apocalypse that it is 'a marvellous portrait of the great god-opposing power that should hereafter arise, who was to exalt might above right, and attempt, successfully or unsuccessfully for the time, to seize the sovereignty of the world, backed by hosts of intellectual workers, who would uphold all his pretensions, justify all his actions, and enforce his political aims by an economic warfare, which menaced with destruction all that did not bow down to his arrogant and godless claims. And though the justness of this forecast is clear to the student who approaches the subject with some insight, and to all students who approach it with the experience of the present world war, we find that as late as 1908, Bousset in his article on the "Antichrist" in Hastings's *Encyclopaedia of Religion and Ethics*, writes as follows: "The interest in the (Antichrist) legend ... is now to be found only among the lower classes of the Christian community, among sects, eccentric individuals, and fanatics."

'No great prophecy receives its full and final fulfilment in any single event, or single series of events. In fact, it may not be fulfilled at all in regard to the object against which it was primarily delivered by the prophet or seer. But, if it is the expression of a great moral and spiritual truth, it will of a surety be fulfilled at sundry times and in divers manners and in varying degrees of completeness. The present attitude of the Central Powers of Europe on this question of might against right, of Caesarism against religion, of the state against God, is the greatest fulfilment that the Johannine prophecy in XIII has as yet received. Even the very indefiniteness regarding the chief Antichrist in XIII is reproduced in the present upheaval of evil powers. In XIII the Antichrist is conceived as a single individual, i.e., the demonic Nero; but even so, behind him stands the Roman Empire, which is one with him in character and purpose, and in itself the Fourth Kingdom or the Kingdom of the Antichrist—in fact, the Antichrist itself. So in regard to the present war, it is difficult to determine whether the Kaiser or his people can advance the best claims to the title of a modern Antichrist. If he is a present-day representative of the Antichrist, so just as surely is the empire behind him, for it is one in spirit and purpose with its leader—whether regarded from its military side, its intellectual, or its industrial. They are in a degree far transcending that of ancient Rome "those who are destroying the earth".'

So there we have Antichrist talking German to Archdeacon Charles, who, at the same moment, is using the books of German scholars for his work on the Apocalypse. It is as if Christianity and ethnological science alike could not exist unless they had an opposite, an Antichrist or an Urdummheit, for an offset. The Antichrist and the Urdummheit are just the fellow who is different from me. Today Antichrist speaks Russian, a hundred years ago he spoke French, tomorrow he may speak cockney or the Glasgow brogue. As for Urdummheit, he speaks any language that isn't Oxford or Harvard or an obsequious imitation of one of these.

CHAPTER VII

IT is childish. What we have now to admit is that the beginning of the new era (our own) coincided with the dying of the old era of the true pagans or, in the Greek sense, barbarians. As our present civilisation was showing the first sparks of life, say in 1000 B.C., the great and ancient civilisation of the older was waning: the great river civilisations of the Euphrates, the Nile, and the Indus, with the lesser sea-civilisations of the Aegean. It is puerile to deny the age and the greatness of the three river civilisations, with their intermediary cultures in Persia or Iran, and in the Aegean, Crete or Mycenae. That any of these civilisations could do a sum in long division we do not pretend. They may not even have invented the wheel-barrow. A modern child of ten could lick them hollow in arithmetic, geometry, or even, maybe, astronomy. And what of it?

What of it? Because they lacked our modern mental and mechanical attainments, were they any less 'civilised' or 'cultured', the Egyptians and the Chaldeans, the Cretans and the Persians and the Hindus of the Indus, than we are? Let us look at a great seated statue of Rameses, or at Etruscan tombs; let us read of Assiburnipal or Darius, and then say: How do our modern factory-workers show beside the delicate Egyptian friezes of the common people of Egypt? or our khaki soldiers, beside the Assyrian friezes? or our Trafalgar Square lions beside these of Mycenae? Civilisation? it is revealed rather in sensitive life than in inventions: and have we anything as good as the Egyptians of two or three thousand years before Christ as a people? Culture and civilisation are tested by vital consciousness. Are we more vitally conscious than an Egyptian 3000 years B.C. was? Are we? Probably we are less. Our conscious range is wide, but shallow as a sheet of paper. We have no depth to our consciousness.

A rising thing is a passing thing, says Buddha. A rising civilisation is a passing civilisation. Greece rose upon the passing of the Aegean : and the Aegean was the link between Egypt and Babylon. Greece rose as the passing of the Aegean civilisation, and Rome rose as the same, for the Etruscan civilisation was a last strong wave from the Aegean, and Rome rose, truly, from the Etruscans. Persia arose from between the cultures of the Euphrates and the Indus, and no doubt, in the passing of these.

Perhaps every rising civilisation must fiercely repudiate the passing civilisation. It is a fight within the self. The Greeks fiercely repudiated the barbarians. But we know now, the barbarians of the east Mediterranean were as much Greeks as most of the Greeks themselves. They were only Greeks, or autochthonous Hellenes who adhered to the old way of culture instead of taking on the new. The Aegean must always have been, in the primitive sense, Hellenic. But the old Aegean culture is different from what we call Greek, especially in its religious basis. Every old civilisation, we may be certain of it, had a definitely religious basis. The nation was, in a very old sense, a church, or a vast cult-unit. From cult to culture is only a step, but it took a lot of making. Cult-lore was the wisdom of the old races. We now have culture.

It is fairly difficult for one culture to understand another. But for culture to understand cult-lore is extremely difficult, and, for rather stupid people, impossible. Because culture is chiefly an activity of the mind, and cult-lore is an activity of the senses. The pre-Greek ancient world had not the faintest inkling of the lengths to which mental activity could be carried. Even Pythagoras, whoever he was, had no inkling: nor Herakleitos nor even Empedokles or Anaxagoras. Socrates and Aristotle were the first to *perceive* the dawn.

But on the other hand, we have not the faintest conception of the vast range that was covered by the ancient sense-consciousness. We have lost almost entirely the great and intricately developed sensual awareness, or sense-awareness, and sense-knowledge, of the ancients. It was a great depth of knowledge arrived at direct, by instinct and intuition, as we say, not by reason. It was a knowledge based not on words but on images. The abstraction was not into generalisations or into qualities, but into symbols. And the connection was not logical but emotional. The word 'therefore' did not exist. Images or symbols succeeded one another in a procession of instinctive and arbitrary physical connection—some of the Psalms give us examples—and they 'get nowhere' because there was nowhere to get to, the desire was to achieve a consummation of a certain state of consciousness, to fulfil a certain state of feeling-awareness. Perhaps all that remains to us today of the ancient way of 'thought-process' are games like chess and cards. Chess-men and card-figures are symbols: their 'values' are fixed in each case: their 'movements' are non-logical, arbitrary, and based on the power-instinct.

Not until we can grasp a little of the working of the ancient mind can we appreciate the 'magic' of the world they lived in. Take even the sphinx conundrum: *What is it that goes first on four legs, then on two, and then on three?* —The answer is: Man.—To us it is rather silly, the great question of the sphinx. But in the uncritical ancient who *felt* his images, there would spring up a great complex of emotions and fears. The thing that goes on four legs is the animal, in all its animal difference and potency, its hinterland consciousness which circles round the isolated consciousness of man. And when, in the answer, it is shown that the baby goes on four legs, instantly there springs up another emotional complex, half fear, half amusement, as man realises himself as an animal, especially in the infantile state, going on all fours with face to the ground and belly or navel polarised to the earth's centre, like a true animal, instead of navel polarised to the sun, as in the true man, according to primitive conception. The second clause, of the two-legged creature, would bring up complex images of men, monkeys, birds, and frogs, and the weird falling into relationship of these four would be an instant imaginative act, such as is very hard for us to achieve, but which children still make. The last clause, of the three-legged creature, would bring wonder, faint terror, and a searching of the great hinterlands beyond the deserts and the sea for some still-unrevealed beast.

So we see that the emotional reaction to such a conundrum was enormous. And even kings and heroes like Hector or Menelaus would make the same reaction, as a child now does, but a thousandfold stronger and wider. Men were not fools for so doing. Men are far more fools today, for stripping themselves of their emotional and imaginative reactions, and feeling nothing. The price we pay is boredom and deadness. Our bald processes of thought no longer are life to us. For the sphinx-riddle of man is as terrifying today as it was before Oedipus, and more so. For now it is the riddle of the dead-alive man, which it never was before.

CHAPTER VIII

MAN thought and still thinks in images. But now our images have hardly any emotional value. We always want a 'conclusion', an end, we always want to come, in our mental processes, to a decision, a finality, a full stop. This gives us a sense of satisfaction. All our mental consciousness is a movement onwards, a movement in stages, like our sentences, and every full-stop is a mile-stone that marks our 'progress' and our arrival somewhere. On and on we go, for the mental consciousness. Whereas of course there is no goal. Consciousness is an end in itself. We torture ourselves getting somewhere, and when we get there it is nowhere, for there is nowhere to get to.

While men still thought of the heart or the liver as the seat of consciousness, they had no idea of this on-and-on process of thought. To them a thought was a completed state of feeling-awareness, a cumulative thing, a deepening thing, in which feeling deepened into feeling in consciousness till there was a sense of fulness. A completed thought was the plumbing of a depth like a whirlpool, of emotional awareness, and at the depth of this whirlpool of emotion the resolve formed. But it was no stage in a journey. There was no logical chain to be dragged further.

This should help us to appreciate that the oracles were not supposed to say something that fitted plainly in the whole chain of circumstance. They were supposed to deliver a set of images or symbols of the real dynamic value, which should set the emotional consciousness of the enquirer, as he pondered them, revolving more and more rapidly, till out of a state of intense emotional absorption the resolve at last formed; or, as we say, the decision was arrived at. As a matter of fact, we do very much the same in a crisis. When anything very important is to be decided we withdraw and ponder and ponder until the deep emotions are

set working and revolving together, revolving, revolving,
till a centre is formed and we 'know what to do'. And the
fact that no politician today has the courage to follow
this intensive method of 'thought' is the reason of the
absolute paucity of the political mind today.

CHAPTER IX

WELL then, let us return to the Apocalypse with this in mind: that the Apocalypse is still, in its movement, one of the works of the old pagan civilisation, and in it we have, not the modern process of progressive thought, but the old pagan process of rotary image-thought. Every image fulfils its own little circle of action and meaning, then is superseded by another image. This is specially so in the first part, before the birth of the Child. Every image is a picturegraph, and the connection between the images will be made more or less differently by every reader. Nay, every image will be understood differently by every reader, according to his emotion-reaction. And yet there is a certain precise plan or scheme.

We must remember that the old human conscious process has to *see something happen*, every time. Everything is concrete, there are no abstractions. And everything *does* something.

To the ancient consciousness, Matter, Materia, or Substantial things are God. A pool of water is god. And why not? The longer we live the more we return to the oldest of all visions. A great rock *is* god. I can touch it. It is undeniable. It is god.

Then those things that move are doubly god. That is, we are doubly aware of their godhead: that which is, and that which moves is twice godly. Everything is a 'thing': and every 'thing' acts and has effect: the universe is a great complex activity of things existing and moving and having effect. And all this is god.

Today, it is almost impossible for us to realise what the old Greeks meant by god, or *theos*. Everything was *theos*; but even so, not at the same moment. At the moment, whatever *struck* you was god. If it was a pool of water, the very watery pool might strike you: then that was god; or a faint vapour at evening rising might catch the imagination: then that was *theos*; or thirst might overcome you at the sight of the water: then the thirst itself was god; or you drank, and the delicious and indescribable slaking of thirst was the god; or you felt the sudden chill of the water as you touched it: and then another god came into being, 'the cold': and this was not a *quality*, it was an existing entity, almost a creature, certainly a *theos*: the cold; or again, on the dry lips something suddenly alighted: it was 'the moist', and again a god. Even to the early scientists or philosophers, 'the cold', 'the moist', 'the hot', 'the dry' were things in themselves, realities, gods, *theoi*. And they *did things*.

With the coming of Socrates and 'the spirit', the cosmos died. For two thousand years man has been living in a dead or dying cosmos, hoping for a heaven hereafter. And all the religions have been religions of the dead body and the postponed reward: eschatological, to use a pet word of the philosophers.

It is very difficult for us to understand the pagan mind. When we are given translations of stories from the ancient Egyptian, the stories are almost entirely unintelligible. It may be the translations' fault: who can pretend really to *read* hieroglyph script! But when we are given translations from Bushman folk-lore, we find ourselves in almost the same puzzled state. The words may be intelligible, but the connection between them is impossible to follow. Even when we read translations of Hesiod, or even of Plato, we feel that a meaning has been arbitrarily *given* to the movement that is wrong, the inner connection. Flatter ourselves as we may, the gulf between Professor Jowett's mentality and Plato's mentality is almost impassable; and Professor Jowett's Plato is, in the end, just Professor Jowett with hardly a breath of the living Plato. Plato divorced from his great pagan background is really only another Victorian statue in a toga—or a chlamys.

To get at the Apocalypse we have to appreciate the mental working of the pagan thinker or poet—pagan thinkers were necessarily poets—who starts with an image, sets the image in motion, allows it to achieve a certain course or circuit of its own, and then takes up another image. The old Greeks were very fine image-thinkers, as the myths prove. Their images were wonderfully natural and harmonious. They followed the logic of action rather than of reason, and they had no moral axe to grind. But still they are nearer to us than the orientals, whose image-thinking often followed no plan whatsoever, not even the sequence of action. We can see it in some of the Psalms, the flitting from image to image with no essential connection at all, but just the curious image-association. The oriental loved that.

To appreciate the pagan manner of thought we have to drop our own manner of on-and-on-and-on, from a start to a finish, and allow the mind to move in cycles, or to flit here and there over a cluster of images. Our idea of time as a continuity in an eternal straight line has crippled our consciousness cruelly. The pagan conception of time as moving in cycles is much freer, it allows movement upwards and downwards, and allows for a complete change of the state of mind, at any moment. One cycle finished, we can drop or rise to another level, and be in a new world at once. But by our time-continuum method, we have to trail wearily on over another ridge.

The old method of the Apocalypse is to set forth the image, make a world, and then suddenly depart from this world in a cycle of time and movement and event, an *epos*; and then return again to a world not quite like the original one, but on another level. The 'world' is established on twelve: the number twelve is basic for an established cosmos. And the cycles move in sevens.

This old plan still remains, but very much broken up. The Jews always spoilt the beauty of a plan by forcing some ethical or tribal meaning in. The Jews have a moral instinct against design. Design, lovely plan, is pagan and immoral. So that we are not surprised, after the experience of Ezekiel and Daniel, to find the *mise en scène* of the vision muddled up, Jewish temple furniture shoved in, and twenty-four elders or presbyters who no longer quite know what they are, but are trying to be as Jewish as possible, and so on. The sea as of glass has come in from the Babylonian cosmos, the bright waters of heaven, as contrasted with the bitter or dead waters of the earthly sea: but of course it has to be put in a dish, a temple laver. Everything Jewish is *interior*. Even the stars of heaven and the waters of the fresh firmament have to be put inside the curtains of that stuffy tabernacle or temple.

But whether John of Patmos actually left the opening vision of the throne and the four starry creatures and the twenty-four elders or witnesses in the muddle we find them in, or whether later editors deliberately, in true Christian spirit, broke up the design, we don't know. John of Patmos was a Jew, so he didn't much mind whether his vision was imaginable or not. But even then, we feel the Christian scribes smashed up the pattern, to 'make it safe'. Christians have always been 'making things safe'.

The book had difficulty in getting into the Bible at all: the eastern Fathers objected to it so strongly. So if, in Cromwellian fashion, the heathen figures had their noses and heads knocked off, to 'make them safe', we can't wonder. All we can do is to remember that there is probably a pagan kernel to the book: that this was written over, perhaps more than once, by Jewish apocalyptists, before the time of Christ: that John of Patmos probably wrote over the whole book once more, to make it Christian: and after that, Christian scribes and editors tinkered with it to make it safe. They could go on tinkering for more than a hundred years.

Once we allow for pagan symbols more or less distorted by the Jewish mind and the Christian iconoclast, and for Jewish temple and ritual symbols arbitrarily introduced to make the heavens fit inside that precious Israelitish tabernacle, we can get a fairly good idea of the *mise en scène*, the vision of the throne with the cosmic beasts giving praise, and the rainbow-shrouded Kosmokrator about whose presence the prismatic glory glows like a rainbow and a cloud: 'Iris too is a cloud'. This Kosmokrator gleams with the colour of jasper and the sardine stone: the commentators say greenish yellow, whereas in Ezekiel it was amber yellow, as the effulgence of the cosmic fire. Jasper equates with the sign *Pisces*, which is the astrological sign of our era. Only now are we passing over the border of Pisces, into a new sign and a new era. And Jesus was called The Fish, for the same reason, during the first centuries. Such a powerful hold had star-lore, originally Chaldean, over the mind of man!

From the throne proceed thunders and lightnings and

voices. Thunder indeed was the first grand cosmic utterance.
It was a being in itself: another aspect of the Almighty
or the Demiurge: and its voice was the first great cosmic
noise, betokening creation. The grand Logos of the beginning was a thunderclap laughing throughout chaos, and
causing the cosmos. But the thunder, which is also the
Almighty, and the lightning, which is the Fiery Almighty,
putting forth the first jet of life-flame—the fiery Logos—
have both also their angry or sundering aspect. Thunder
claps creative through space, lightning darts in fecund fire:
or the reverse, destructive.

Then before the throne are the seven lamps, which are
explained as the seven Spirits of God. Explanations are
fishy, in a work like this. But the seven lamps are the seven
planets (including sun and moon) who are the seven Rulers
from the heavens over the earth and over us. The great
sun that makes day and makes all life on earth, the moon that
sways the tides and sways our physical being, unknown,
sways the menstrual period in women and the sexual
rhythm in a man, then the five big wandering stars, Mars,
Venus, Saturn, Jupiter, Mercury, these, which are also our
days of the week, are as much our Rulers now as ever they
were: and as little. We know we live by the sun: how
much we live by the others, we don't know. We reduce it
all to simple gravitation-pull. Even at that, strange fine
threads hold us to the moon and stars. That these threads
have a psychic pull on us, we know from the moon. But
what of the stars? How can we say? We have lost that sort
of awareness.

However, we have the *mise en scène* of the drama of the
Apocalypse—call it heaven, if you like. It really means the
complete cosmos as we now have it: the 'unregenerate'
cosmos.

The Almighty had a book in his hand. The book is no
doubt a Jewish symbol. They were a bookish people: and
always great keepers of accounts: reckoning up sins
throughout the ages. But the Jewish symbol of a book will
do fairly well, with its seven seals, to represent a cycle of
seven: though how the book is to be *opened* piece by piece,
after the breaking of each seal, I myself cannot see: since
the book is a rolled up scroll, and therefore could not
actually be opened till all seven seals were broken. However,

it is a detail: to the apocalyptist and to me. Perhaps there is no intention of opening it, till the end.

The Lion of Judah is supposed to open the book. But lo! when the kingly beast comes on to the stage, it turns out to be a Lamb with seven horns (of power, the seven powers or potencies) and seven eyes (the same old planets). We are always hearing a terrific roaring as of lions, and we are always seeing a Lamb exhibiting this wrath. John of Patmos' Lamb is, we suspect, the good old lion in sheep's clothing. It behaves like the most terrific lion. Only John insists that it is a Lamb.

He has to insist on the Lamb, in spite of his predilection for lions, because Leo must now give way to Aries; for, throughout the whole world, the God who, like a lion, was given blood sacrifice must be shoved into the background, and the sacrificed god must occupy the foreground. The pagan mysteries of the sacrifice of the god for the sake of a greater resurrection are older than Christianity, and on one of these mysteries the Apocalypse is based. A Lamb it has to be: or with Mithras, a bull: and the blood drenches over the initiate from the cut throat of the bull (they lifted his head up as they cut his throat) and makes him a new man.

> 'Wash me in the blood of the Lamb
> And I shall be whiter than snow——'

shrieks the Salvation Army in the market place. How surprised they would be if you told them it might just as well have been a bull. But perhaps they wouldn't. They might twig at once. In the lowest stratum of society religion remains pretty much the same, throughout the ages.

(But when it was for a hecatomb, they held the head of the bull downwards, to earth, and cut his throat over a pit. We feel that John's Lamb was for a hecatomb.)

God became the animal that was slain, instead of the animal that does the slaying. With the Jews, then, it had to be a Lamb, partly because of their ancient paschal sacrifice. The Lion of Judah put on a fleece: but by their bite ye shall know them. John insists on a Lamb 'as it were slain': but we never see it slain, we only see it slaying mankind by the million. Even when it comes on in a victorious bloody shirt at the end, the blood is not its *own* blood: it is the blood of inimical kings.

> 'Wash me in the blood of my enemies
> And I shall be that I am——'

says John of Patmos in effect.

There follows a paean. What it is, is a real pagan paean of praise to the god who is about to demonstrate—the elders, those twice twelve of the established cosmos, who are really the twelve signs of the zodiac on their 'seats', keep getting up and bowing to the throne, like the sheaves to Joseph. Vials of sweet odour are labelled: Prayers of the saints; probably an aftertouch of some little Christian later on. Flocks of Jewish angels flock in. And then the drama begins.

CHAPTER X

WITH the famous four horsemen, the real drama begins. These four horsemen are obviously pagan. They are not even Jewish. In they ride, one after the other—though why they should come from the opening of the seals of a *book*, we don't know. In they ride, short and sharp, and it is over. They have been cut down to a minimum.

But there they are: obviously astrological, zodiacal, prancing in to a purpose. To what purpose? This time, really individual and human, rather than cosmic. The famous book of seven seals in this place is the body of man: of a man: of Adam: of any man: and the seven seals are the seven centres or gates of his dynamic consciousness. We are witnessing the opening and conquest of the great psychic centres of the human body. The old Adam is going to be conquered, die, and be reborn as the new Adam: but in stages: in sevenfold stages: or in six stages, and then a climax, seven. For man has seven levels of awareness, deeper and higher: or seven spheres of consciousness. And one by one these must be conquered, transformed, transfigured.

And what are these seven spheres of consciousness in a man? Answer as you please, any man can give his own answer. But taking common 'popular' view they are, shall we say, the four dynamic natures of man and the three 'higher' natures. Symbols mean something: yet they mean something different to every man. Fix the meaning of a symbol, and you have fallen into the commonplace of allegory.

Horses, always horses! How the horse dominated the mind of the early races, especially of the Mediterranean! You were a lord if you had a horse. Far back, far back in our dark soul the horse prances. He is a dominant symbol: he gives us lordship: he links us, the first palpable and throbbing link with the ruddy-glowing Almighty of potence: he is the beginning even of our godhead in the flesh. And as a symbol he roams the dark underworld meadows of the soul. He stamps and threshes in the dark fields of your soul and of mine. The sons of God who came down and knew the daughters of men and begot the great Titans, they had 'the members of horses', says Enoch.

Within the last fifty years man has lost the horse. Now man is lost. Man is lost to life and power—an underling and a wastrel. While horses thrashed the streets of London, London lived.

The horse, the horse! the symbol of surging potency and power of movement, of action, in man. The horse, that heroes strode. Even Jesus rode an ass, a mount of humble power. But the horse for true heroes. And different horses for the different powers, for the different heroic flames and impulses.

The rider on the white horse! Who is he then? The man who needs an explanation will never know. Yet explanations are our doom.

Take the old four natures of man: the sanguine, the choleric, the melancholic, the phlegmatic! There you have the four colours of the horses, white, red, black, and *pale*, or yellowish. But how should sanguine be white?—Ah, because the blood was the life itself, the very life: and the very power of life itself was white, dazzling. In our old days, *the blood was the life*, and visioned as power it was like white light. The scarlet and the purple were only the clothing of the blood. Ah, the vivid blood clothed in bright red! itself it was like pure light.

The red horse is choler: not mere anger, but natural fieriness, what we call passion.

The black horse was the black bile, refractory.

And the phlegm, or lymph of the body was the pale horse: in excess it causes death, and is followed by Hades.

Or take the four planetary natures of man: jovial, martial, saturnine, and mercurial. This will do for another correspondence, if we go a little behind the *Latin* meaning, to the older Greek. Then Great Jove is the sun, and the living blood: the white horse: and angry Mars rides the red horse: Saturn is black, stubborn, refractory and gloomy: and Mercury is really Hermes, Hermes of the Underworld, the guide of souls, the watcher over two ways, the opener of two doors, he who seeks through hell, or Hades.

There are two sets of correspondence, both physical. We leave the cosmic meanings, for the intention here is more physical than cosmic.

You will meet the white horse over and over again, as a symbol. Does not even Napoleon have a white horse? The old meanings control our actions, even when our minds have gone inert.

But the rider on the white horse is crowned. He is the royal me, he is my very self and his horse is the whole *mana* of a man. He is my very me, my sacred ego, called into a new cycle of action by the Lamb and riding forth to conquest, the conquest of the old self for the birth of a new self. It is he, truly, who shall conquer all the other 'powers' of the self. And he rides forth, like the sun, with arrows, to conquest, but not with the sword, for the sword implies also judgment, and this is my dynamic or potent self. And his bow is the bended bow of the body, like the crescent moon.

The true action of the myth, or ritual-imagery, has been all cut away. The rider on the white horse appears, then vanishes. But we know why he has appeared. And we know why he is paralleled at the end of the Apocalypse by the last rider on the white horse, who is the heavenly Son of Man riding forth after the last and final conquest over the 'kings'. The son of man, even you or I, rides forth to the small conquest: but the Great Son of Man mounts his white horse after the last universal conquest, and leads on his hosts. His shirt is red with the blood of monarchs, and on his thigh is his title: King of Kings and Lord of Lords. (Why on his thigh? Answer for yourself. Did not Pythagoras show his golden thigh in the temple? Don't you know the old and powerful Mediterranean symbol of the thigh?) But out of the mouth of the final rider on the white horse comes that fatal sword of the logos of judgment. Let us go back to the bow and arrows of him to whom judgment is not given.

The myth has been cut down to the bare symbols. The first rider only rides forth. After the second rider, peace is lost, strife and war enter the world—really the inner world of the self. After the rider on the black horse, who carries the balances of measure, that weigh out the measures or true proportions of the 'elements' in the body, bread becomes scarce, though wine and oil are not hurt. Bread, barley is here the body or flesh which is symbolically sacrificed—as in the barley scattered over the victim in a Greek sacrifice: 'Take this bread of my body with thee.' The body of flesh is now at famine stage, wasted down. Finally, with the rider on the pale horse, the last, the physical or dynamic self is dead in the 'little death' of the initiate, and we enter the Hades or underworld of our being.

We enter the Hades or underworld of our being, for our body is now 'dead'. But the powers or demons of this underworld can only hurt a fourth part of the earth: that is, a fourth part of the body of flesh: which means, the death is only mystical, and that which is hurt is only the body that belongs to already-established creation. Hunger and physical woes befall the physical body in this little death, but there is as yet no greater hurt. There are no plagues: these are divine wrath, and here we have no anger of the Almighty.

There is a crude and superficial explanation of the four horsemen: but probably it hints at the true meaning. The orthodox commentators who talk about famines in the time of Titus or Vespasian may be reading the bit about barley and wheat correctly, according to a late apocalyptist. The *original* meaning, which was pagan, is smeared over intentionally with a meaning that can fit this 'Church of Christ versus the wicked Gentile Powers' business. But none of that touches the horsemen themselves. And perhaps here better than anywhere else in the book can we see the peculiar way in which the old meaning has been cut away and confused and changed, deliberately, while the bones of the structure have been left.

But there are three more seals. What happens when these are opened?

After the fourth seal and the rider on the pale horse, the initiate, in pagan ritual, is bodily dead. There remains, however, the journey through the underworld, where the living 'I' must divest itself of soul and spirit, before it can at last emerge naked from the far gate of hell into the new day. For the soul, the spirit, and the living 'I' are the three divine natures of man. The four bodily natures are put off on earth. The *two* divine natures can only be divested in Hades. And the last is a stark flame which, on the new day is clothed anew and successively by the spiritual body, the soul-body, and then the 'garment' of flesh, with its fourfold terrestrial natures.

Now no doubt the pagan script recorded this passage through Hades, this divesting of the soul, then of the spirit, till the mystic death is fulfilled sixfold, and the seventh seal is at once the last thunder of death and the first thunderous paean of new birth and tremendous joy.

But the Jewish mind hates the mortal and terrestrial divinity of man: the Christian mind the same. Man is only postponedly divine: when he is dead and gone to glory. He *must not* achieve divinity in the flesh. So the Jewish and Christian apocalyptists abolish the mystery of the individual adventure into Hades and substitute a lot of martyred souls crying under the altar for vengeance—vengeance was a sacred duty with the Jews. These souls are told to wait awhile—always the postponed destiny—until more martyrs are killed; and they are given white robes: which is premature, for the white robes are the new resurrected bodies, and how could these crying souls put them on in Hades: in the grave? However—such is the muddle that Jewish and Christian apocalyptists have made of the fifth seal.

The sixth seal, the divesting of the spirit from the last living quick of the 'I', this has been turned by the apocalyptist into a muddled cosmic calamity. The sun goes black as sackcloth of hair: which means that he is a great black orb streaming forth visible darkness; the moon turns to blood, which is one of the horror-reversals of the pagan mind, for the moon is mother of the watery body of men, the blood belongs to the sun, and the moon, like a harlot or demon woman, can only be drunk with red blood in her utterly maleficent aspect of meretrix, blood-drinker, she who should give the cool water of the body's fountain of flesh; the stars fall from the sky, and the heavens depart like a scroll rolled together, and 'every mountain and island were moved out of their places'. It means the return of chaos, and the end of our cosmic order, or creation. Yet it is not *annihilation*: for the kings of the earth and all the rest of men keep on hiding in the shifted mountains, from the ever-recurrent wrath of the Lamb.

This cosmic calamity no doubt corresponds to the original final death of the initiate, when his very spirit is stripped off him and he knows death indeed, yet still keeps the final flame-point of life, down in Hades. But it is a pity the apocalyptists were so interfering: the Apocalypse is a string of cosmic calamities, monotonous. We would give the New Jerusalem cheerfully, to have back the pagan record of initiation; and this perpetual 'wrath of the Lamb' business exasperates one like endless threats of toothless old men.

However, the six stages of mystic death are over. The seventh stage is a death and birth at once. Then the final flame-point of the eternal self of a man emerges from hell, and at the very instant of extinction becomes a new whole cloven flame, of a new-bodied man with golden thighs and a face of glory. But first there is a pause: a natural pause. The action is suspended, and transferred to another world, to the outer cosmos. There is a lesser cycle of ritual to fulfil, before the seventh seal, the crash and the glory.

CHAPTER XI

CREATION, we know, is four-square, and the number of creation, or of the created universe, is four. From the four corners of the world four winds can blow, three bad winds, one good one. When all the winds are loosed, it means chaos in the air, and destruction on earth.

So the four angels of the winds are told to hold back their winds and hurt neither earth nor sea nor trees: that is, the actual world.

But there is a mystic wind from the east which lifts the sun and the moon like full-sailed ships, and bears them across the sky, like vessels slowly scudding.—This was one of the beliefs, in the second century B.C.—Out of this east rises the angel crying for a pause in the blowing of the winds of destruction, while he shall seal the servants of God in their foreheads. Then the twelve tribes of Jews are tediously enumerated and sealed: a tedious Jewish performance.

The vision changes, and we see a great multitude, clothed in white robes and with palms in their hands, standing before the throne and before the Lamb, and crying with a loud voice: 'Salvation to our God which sitteth upon the throne, and to the Lamb.' Thereupon angels and elders and the four winged beasts fall on their faces and worship God saying: 'Blessing, and glory, and wisdom, and thanksgiving, and honour, and power, and might be unto our God for ever and ever. Amen.'

This suggests that the seventh seal is opened. The angel cries to the four winds to be still, while the blessed, or the new-born appear. And then those who 'went through the great tribulation', or initiation into death and rebirth, appear in glory, clothed in the white dazzling robes of their new bodies, carrying branches of the tree of life in their hands, and appearing in a grand blaze of light before the Almighty.

They hymn their praise, and the angels take it up.

Here we can see, in spite of the apocalyptist, the pagan initiate, perhaps in a temple of Cybele, suddenly brought forth from the underdark of the temple into the grand blaze of light in front of the pillars. Dazzled, reborn, he wears white robes and carries the palm-branch, and the flutes sound out their rapture round him, and dancing women lift their garlands over him. The lights flash, the incense rolls up, the brilliant priests and priestesses throw up their arms and sing the hymn to the new glory of the reborn, as they form around him and exalt him in a kind of ecstasy. The crowd beyond is breathless.

This vivid scene in front of the temple, of the glorification of a new initiate and his identification or assimilation to the god, amid grand brilliance and wonder, and the sound of flutes and the swaying of garlands, in front of the awed crowd of onlookers was, we know, the end of the ritual of the Mysteries of Isis. Such a scene has been turned by the apocalyptists into a Christian vision. But it really takes place *after* the opening of the seventh seal. The cycle of individual initiation is fulfilled. The great conflict and conquest is over. The initiate is dead, and alive again in a new body. He is sealed in the forehead, like a Hindu monk, as a sign that he has died the death, and that his seventh self is fulfilled, he is twice-born, his mystic eye or 'third eye' is now open. He sees in two worlds. Or, like the Pharaohs with the serpent Uraeus rearing between their brows, he has charge of the last proud power of the sun.

But all this is pagan and impious. No Christian is allowed to rise up new and in a divine body, here on earth and in the midst of life. So we are given a crowd of martyrs in heaven, instead.

The seal in the forehead may be ashes: the seal of the death of the body: or it may be scarlet or glory, the new light or vision. It is, really, in itself the seventh seal.

Now it is finished, and there is silence in heaven for the space of about half an hour.

CHAPTER XII

AND here, perhaps, the oldest pagan manuscript ended. At any rate the first cycle of the drama is over. With various hesitations, some old apocalyptist starts the second cycle, this time the cycle of the death and regeneration of earth or world, instead of the individual. And this part, too, we feel is much older than John of Patmos. Nevertheless, it is very Jewish, the curious distortion of paganism through the Jewish moral and cataclysmic vision: the monomaniacal insistence on punishment and woes, which goes right through the Apocalypse. We are now in a real Jewish atmosphere.

But still there are old pagan ideas. Incense rises up to the nostrils of the Almighty in great clouds of smoke. But these clouds of incense-smoke are allegorised, and made to carry up the prayers of the saints. Then the divine fire is cast down to earth, to start the little death and final regeneration of the world, the earth and the multitude. Seven angels, the seven angels of the seven dynamic natures of God, are given seven trumpets to make seven annunciations.

And then the now-Jewish Apocalypse starts to unroll its second cycle of the Seven Trumps.

There is again a division into four and three. We are witnessing the death (the little death) of the cosmos at divine command, and therefore each time there is a trumpet blast, a third part, not a fourth, of the world is destroyed. The divine number is three: the number of the world, four-square, is four.

At the first Trump, a third part of vegetable life is destroyed.

At the second Trump, a third part of all marine life, even ships.

At the third Trump, a third part of the fresh waters of earth are embittered and become poison.

At the fourth Trump, a third part of the heavens, sun, moon, and stars, are destroyed.

This corresponds to the four horsemen of the first cycle, in a clumsy Jewish-apocalyptic parallel. The *material* cosmos has now suffered the little death.

What follows are the 'three woes', which affect the spirit and soul of the world (symbolised now as men), instead of the material part. A star falls to earth: Jewish figure for an angel descending. He has the key of the abyss: Jewish counterpart of Hades. And the action now moves to the underworld of the cosmos instead of the underworld of the self, as in the first cycle.

It is now all Jewish and allegorical, not symbolical any more. The sun and the moon are darkened because we are in the underworld.

The abyss, like the underworld, is full of malefic powers, injurious to man.

For the abyss, like the underworld, represents the superseded powers of creation.

The old nature of man must yield and give way to a new nature. In yielding, it passes away down into Hades, and there lives on, undying and malefic, superseded, yet malevolent-potent in the underworld.

This very profound truth was embodied in all old religions, and lies at the root of the worship of the underworld powers. The worship of the underworld powers, the chthonioi, was perhaps the very basis of the most ancient Greek religion. When man has neither the strength to subdue his underworld powers—which are really the ancient powers of his old, superseded self; nor the wit to placate them with sacrifice and the burnt holocaust; then they come back at him, and destroy him again. Hence every new conquest of life means a 'harrowing of Hell'.

In the same way, after every great cosmic change, the power of the *old* cosmos, superseded, becomes demonic and harmful to the new creation. It is a great truth which lies behind the Gea-Ouranos-Kronos-Zeus series of myths.

Therefore the whole cosmos has its malefic aspect. The sun, the great sun, in so far as he is the *old* sun of a superseded cosmic day, is hateful and malevolent to the new-born, tender thing I am. He does me harm, in my struggling self, for he still has power over my old self and he is hostile.

Likewise the waters of the cosmos, in their *oldness* and their superseded or abysmal nature, are malevolent to life, especially to the life of man. The great Moon and mother of my inner water-streams, in so far as she is the old, dead moon, is hostile, hurtful, and hateful to my flesh, for she still has a power over my old flesh.

This is the meaning away back of the 'two woes': a very deep meaning, too deep for John of Patmos. The famous locusts of the first woe, which emerge from the abyss at the fifth Trump, are complex but not unintelligible symbols. They do not hurt vegetable earth, only the men who have not the new seal on their foreheads. These men they torture, but cannot kill: for it is the little death. And they can torture only for five months, which is a season, the sun's season, and more or less a third part of the year.

Now these locusts are like horses prepared unto battle, which means, horses, horses, that they are hostile potencies or *powers*.

They have hair as the hair of women: the streaming crest of the sun-powers, or sun-rays.

They have the teeth of the lion: the red lion of the sun in his malefic aspect.

They have faces like men: since they are directed only against the *inward* life of men.

They have crowns like gold: they are royal, of the royal orb of the sun.

They have stings in their tails: which means they are in the reversed or hellish aspect, creatures which once were good, but being superseded, of a past order, are now reversed and hellish, stinging, as it were, backwards.

And their king is Apollyon: which is Apollo, great Lord of the (pagan and therefore hellish) sun.

Having made his weird, muddled composite symbol at last intelligible, the Jewish apocalyptist declares the first woe is past, and that there are two more still to come.

CHAPTER XIII

THE sixth Trump sounds. The voice from the golden altar says: Loose the four angels which are bound in the great river Euphrates——

These are evidently four angels of four corners, like those of the four winds. So Euphrates, the evil river of Babylon, will no doubt stand for the waters under the earth, or the abysmal under-ocean, in its hellish aspect.

And the angels are loosed, whereupon, apparently the great army of demon-horsemen, two hundred million, all told, issue from the abyss.

The horses of the two hundred million horsemen have heads as the heads of lions, and out of their mouths issue fire and brimstone. And these kill a third part of men, by the fire, smoke, and brimstone which come out of their mouths. Then unexpectedly we are told that their power is in their mouths and in their tails; for their tails are like serpents, and have heads, and with them they do hurt.

These weird creatures are apocalyptic images, surely: not symbols but personal images of some old apocalyptist long before John of Patmos. The horses are powers, and divine instruments of woe: for they kill a third part of men, and later we are told they are plagues. Plagues are the whips of God.

Now they ought to be the reversed or malevolent powers of the abysmal or underworld waters. Instead of which they are sulphurous, evidently volcanic beasts of the abysmal or underworld fires, which are the hellish fires of the hellish sun.

Then suddenly they are given serpent tails, and they have evil power in their tails. Here we are back at the right thing—the horse-bodied serpent-monster of the salty deeps of hell: the powers of the underworld waters seen in their reversed aspect, malevolent, striking a third of men,

probably with some watery and deadly disease; as the
locusts of the fifth Trump smote men with some hot and
agonising, yet not deadly disease, which ran for a certain
number of months.

So that here probably two apocalyptists have been at
work. The later one did not understand the scheme. He put
in his brimstone horses with their riders having breastplates
of fire and jacinth and brimstone (red, dark blue, and yellow), following his own gay fancy, and perhaps influenced
by some volcanic disturbance and some sight of splendid
red, blue, and yellow cavalry of the east. That is a true
Jewish method.

But then he had to come back to the old manuscript, with
serpent-tailed watery monsters. So he tacked on the serpent
tails to his own horses, and let them gallop.

This apocalyptist of the brimstone horses is probably
responsible for the 'lake of fire burning with brimstone'
into which the souls of fallen angels and wicked men are
cast to burn for ever and ever more. This pleasant place is
the prototype of the Christian hell, specially invented by
the Apocalypse. The old Jewish hells of Sheol and Gehenna
were fairly mild, uncomfortable abysmal places like Hades,
and when a New Jerusalem was created from heaven, they
disappeared. They were part of the old cosmos, and did not
outlast the old cosmos. They were not eternal.

This was not good enough for the brimstone apocalyptist
and John of Patmos. They must have a marvellous, terrific
lake of sulphurous fire that could burn for ever and ever,
so that the souls of the enemy could be kept writhing.
When, after the last Judgment, earth and sky and all creation were swept away, and only glorious heaven remained,
still, away down, there remained this burning lake of fire
in which the souls were suffering. Brilliant glorious eternal
heaven above: and brilliant sulphurous torture-lake away
below. This is the vision of eternity of all Patmossers. They
could not be happy in heaven unless they *knew* their
enemies were unhappy in hell.

And this vision was specially brought into the world
with the Apocalypse. It did not exist before.

Before, the waters of the hellish underworld were bitter
like the sea. They were the evil aspect of the waters under
the earth, which were conceived as some wondrous lake

of sweet, lovely water, source of all the springs and streams of earth, lying away down below the rocks.

The waters of the abyss were salt like the sea. Salt had a great hold on the old imagination. It was supposed to be the product of 'elemental' injustice. Fire and water, the two great living elements and opposites, gave rise to all substance in their slippery unstable 'marriage'. But when one triumphed over the other, there was 'injustice'. So, when the sun-fire got too strong for the sweet waters, it *burnt* them, and when water was burnt by fire, it produced salt, child of injustice. This child of injustice corrupted the waters and made them bitter. So the sea came into being. And thence the dragon of the sea, leviathan.

And so the bitter waters of hell were the place where souls were drowned: the bitter anti-life ocean of the end.

There was for ages a resentment against the sea: the bitter, corrupt sea, as Plato calls it. But this seems to have died down in Roman times: so our apocalyptist substitutes a brimstone-burning lake, as being more horrific, and able to make the souls suffer more.

A third of men are killed by these brimstone horsemen. But the remaining two-thirds do not refrain from worshipping idols which can 'neither see nor hear nor walk'.

That sounds as if the Apocalypse here was still quite Jewish and pre-Christian. There is no Lamb about.

Later, this second woe winds up with the usual earthquakes. But since the shiver of the earth must immediately give rise to a new movement, it is postponed awhile.

CHAPTER XIV

SIX Trumps are blown, so now there is a pause: just as there was a pause after the Six Seals were opened, to let the angels of the four winds arrange themselves, and the action transfer itself to heaven.

Now, however, come various interruptions. First there comes down a mighty angel, a cosmic lord, something like the Son of Man in the first vision. But the Son of Man, indeed all Messianic reference, seems missing in this part of the Apocalypse. This mighty angel sets one burning foot upon the sea and one on earth, and roars like a lion throughout space. Whereupon the seven creative thunders roll out their creative utterances. These seven thunders, we know, are the seven tonal natures of the Almighty, Maker of heaven and earth: and now they are giving voice to seven vast new commands, for a new cosmic day, a new phase in creation. The seer is in a hurry to write down these seven new words, but he is commanded not to do so. He is not allowed to divulge the nature of the commands which will bring the new cosmos into being. We must wait for the actuality. Then this great 'angel' or cosmic lord raises his hand and swears, by heaven and earth and water under the earth, which is the great Greek oath of the gods, that the old Time is over, the mystery of God is about to be fulfilled.

Then the seer is given the little book to eat. It is the lesser general or universal message of the destruction of the old world and creation of the new: a lesser message than that of the destruction of the old Adam and the creation of new man, which the seven-sealed book told. And it is sweet in the mouth—as revenge is sweet—but bitter in experience.

Then another interruption: the measuring of the temple, a pure Jewish interruption; the measuring or counting of the 'chosen of God', before the end of the old world; and the exclusion of the unchosen.

Then comes the most curious interruption of the two witnesses. Orthodox commentators identify these two witnesses with Moses and Elijah who were with Jesus in the transfiguration on the mount. They are something much older too. These two witnesses are prophets clothed in sackcloth: that is, they are in their woeful aspect, hostile or reversed. They are the two candlesticks and the two olive trees which stand before 'Adonai', the god of the earth. They have power over the waters of the sky (rain), power to turn water into blood, and to smite the earth with all the plagues. They make their testimony, then the beast out of the Abyss rises and slays them. Their dead bodies lie out in the street of the great city, and the people of the earth rejoice because these two who tormented them are dead. But after three and a half days, the spirit of life from God enters the dead two, they rise to their feet, and a great voice says from heaven, 'Come up hither'. So they rise to heaven on a cloud, and their enemies in fear behold them.

It looks as if we had here a layer of very old myth referring to the mysterious twins, 'the little ones', who had such power over the nature of men. But both the Jewish and Christian apocalyptists have balked this bit of Revelation: they have not given it any plain meaning of any sort.

The twins belong to a very old cult which apparently was common to all ancient European peoples; but it seems they were heavenly twins, belonging to the sky. Yet when they were identified by the Greeks with the Tyndarids, Kastor and Polydeukes, already in the Odyssey, they lived alternately in Heaven and in Hades, witnessing to both places. And as such, they may be the candlesticks, or stars of heaven, on the one hand, and the olive trees of the underworld, on the other.

But the older a myth, the deeper it goes in the human consciousness, the more varied will be the forms it takes in the upper consciousness. We have to remember that some symbols, and this of the twins is one of them, can carry even our modern consciousness back for a thousand years, for two thousand years, for three thousand years, for four thousand years, and even beyond that. The power of suggestion is most mysterious. It may not work at all: or it may carry the unconscious mind back in great cyclic swoops through eras of time: or it may go only part way.

If we think of the heroic Dioskouroi, the Greek Twins, the Tyndarids, we go back only halfway. The Greek heroic age did a strange thing, it made every cosmic conception anthropomorphic, yet kept a great deal of the cosmic wonder. So that the Dioskouroi are and are not the ancient twins.

But the Greeks themselves were always reverting to the pre-heroic, pre-Olympian gods and potencies. The Olympic-heroic vision was always felt to be too shallow, the old Greek soul would drop continually to deeper, older, darker levels of religious consciousness, all through the centuries. So that the mysterious Tritopatores at Athens, who were also called the Twins, and Dioskouroi, were the lords of the winds, and mysterious watchers at the procreation of children. So here again we are back in the old levels.

When the Samothracian cult spread in Hellas, in the third and second centuries B.C., then the twins became the *Kabeiroi*, or the Kabiri, and then again they had an enormous suggestive influence over the minds of men. The Kabiri were a swing back to the old idea of the dark or mysterious twins, connected with the movement of the cloudy skies and the air, and with the movement of fertility, and the perpetual and mysterious balance between these two. The apocalyptist sees them in their woeful aspect, masters of sky-water and the waters of earth, which they can turn into blood, and masters of plagues from Hades: the heavenly and hellish aspect of the twins, malevolent.

But the Kabiri were connected with many things: and it is said their cult is still alive in Mohammedan countries. They were the two secret little ones, the homunculi, and the 'rivals'. They were also connected with thunder, and with two round black thunder-stones. So they were called the 'sons of thunder', and had power over rain: also power to curdle milk, and malefic power to turn water into blood. As thunderers they were sunderers, sundering cloud, air, and water. And always they have this aspect of rivals, dividers, separators, for good as well as for ill: balancers.

By another symbolic leap, they were also the ancient gods of gateposts, and then they were the guardians of the gate, and then the twin beasts that guard the altar, or the tree, or the urn, in so many Babylonian, Aegean, and Etruscan

paintings and sculpture. They were often panthers, leopards,
gryphons, earth and night creatures, jealous ones.

It is they who hold things asunder to make a space, a
gateway. In this way, they are rainmakers: they open the
gates in the sky: perhaps as thunder-stones. In the same
way they are the secret lords of sex, for it was early recognised that sex is a holding of two things asunder, that birth
may come through between them. In the sexual sense, they
can change water into blood: for the phallos itself was the
homunculus, and, in one aspect, it was itself the twins of
earth, the small one who made water and the small one
who was filled with blood: the rivals within a man's own
very nature and earthly self symbolised again in the twin
stones of the testes. They are thus the roots of the twin
olive trees, producing the olives, and the oil of the procrea-
tive sperm. They are also the two candlesticks which stand
before the lord of earth, Adonai. For they give the two
alternate forms of elemental consciousness, our day-con-
sciousness and our night-consciousness, that which we are
in the depths of night, and that other very different being
which we are in bright day. A creature of dual and jealous
consciousness is man, and the twins witness jealously to the
duality. Physiologically, in the same meaning, it is they who
hold apart the two streams of the water and of the blood in
our bodies. If the water and blood ever mingled in our
bodies, we should be dead. The two streams are kept apart
by the little ones, the rivals. And on the two streams depends
the dual consciousness.

Now these little ones, these rivals, they are 'witnesses' to
life, for it is between their opposition that the Tree of Life
itself grows, from the earthly root. They testify before the
god of earth or fecundity all the time. And all the time,
they put a limit on man. They say to him, in every earthly
or physical activity: Thus far and no farther.—They limit
every action, every 'earth' action, to its own scope, and
counterbalance it with an opposite action. They are gods of
gates, but they are also gods of limits: each forever jealous
of the other, keeping the other in bounds. They make life
possible; but they make life limited. As the testes, they hold
the phallic balance forever, they are the two phallic witnesses. They are the enemies of intoxication, of ecstasy, and
of licence, of licentious freedom. Always they testify to

Adonai. Hence the men in the cities of licence rejoice when
the beast from the abyss, which is the hellish dragon or
demon of the earth's destruction, or man's bodily destruction, at last kills these two 'guardians', regarded as a sort of
policemen in 'Sodom' and 'Egypt'. The bodies of the slain
two lie unburied for three and a half days: that is half a
week, or half a period of time, when all decency and
restraint has departed from among men.

The language of the text, 'rejoice and make merry and
send gifts to one another' suggests a pagan Saturnalia, like
the Hermaia of Crete or the Sakaia at Babylon, the feast of
unreason. If this is what the apocalyptist meant, it shows
how intimately he follows pagan practice, for the ancient
saturnalian feasts all represented the breaking, or at least
the interruption of an old order of rule and law: and this
time it is the 'natural rule' of the two witnesses which is
broken. Men escape from the laws even of their own nature
for a spell: for three days and a half, which is half the
sacred week, be a 'little' period of time. Then, as heralding
the new earth and the new body of man, the two witnesses
stand up again: men are struck with terror: the voice from
heaven calls the two witnesses, and they go up in a cloud.

'Two, two for the lily-white boys, clothed all in
green-O!——'

Thus the earth, and the body, cannot die its death till
these two sacred twins, the rivals, have been killed.

An earthquake comes, the seventh angel blows his trumpet and makes the great announcement: The kingdoms of
this world are become the kingdoms of our Lord and of his
Christ, and he shall reign for ever and ever.—So there is
again worship and thanksgiving in heaven, that God takes
the reign again. And the temple of God is opened in heaven,
the holy of holies is revealed, and the ark of the testament.
Then there are the lightnings, voices, thunderings, earthquakes, and hail which end a period and herald another.
The third woe is ended.

And here ends the first part of the Apocalypse: the old
half. The little myth that follows stands quite alone in the
book, dramatically, and is really out of keeping with the
rest. One of the apocalyptists put it in as part of a theoretic
scheme: the birth of the Messiah after the little death of
earth and man. And the other apocalyptists left it there.

CHAPTER XVI

THE woman is one of the 'wonders'. And the other wonder is the Dragon. The dragon is one of the oldest symbols of the human consciousness. The dragon and serpent symbol goes so deep in every human consciousness, that a rustle in the grass can startle the toughest 'modern' to depths he has no control over.

First and foremost, the dragon is the symbol of the fluid, rapid, startling movement of life within us. That startled life which runs through us like a serpent, or coils within us potent and waiting, like a serpent, this is the dragon. And the same with the cosmos.

From earliest times, man has been aware of a 'power' or potency within him—and also outside him—which he has no ultimate control over. It is a fluid, rippling potency which can lie quite dormant, sleeping, and yet be ready to leap out unexpectedly. Such are the sudden angers that spring upon us from within ourselves, passionate and terrible in passionate people : and the sudden accesses of violent desire, wild sexual desire, or violent hunger, or a great desire of any sort, even for sleep. The hunger which made Esau sell his birthright would have been called his dragon : later, the Greeks would even have called it a 'god' in him. It is something beyond him, yet within him. It is swift and surprising as a serpent, and overmastering as a dragon. It leaps up from somewhere inside him, and has the better of him.

Primitive man, or shall we say early man, was in a certain sense afraid of his own nature, it was so violent and unexpected inside him, always 'doing things to him'. He early recognised the half-divine, half-demonish nature of this 'unexpected' potency inside him.

Sometimes it came upon him like a glory, as when Samson slew the lion with his hands, or David slew Goliath with a pebble. The Greeks before Homer would have called both these two acts 'the god', in recognition of the superhuman nature of the deed, *and of the doer of the deed* who was *within* the man. This 'doer of the deed', the fluid, rapid, invincible, even clairvoyant potency that can surge through the whole body and spirit of a man, this is the dragon, the grand divine dragon of his superhuman potency, or the great demonish dragon of his inward destruction. It is this which surges in us to make us move, to make us act, to make us bring forth something: to make us spring up and live. Modern philosophers may call it Libido or *Elan Vital*, but the words are thin, they carry none of the wild suggestion of the dragon.

And man 'worshipped' the dragon. A hero was a hero, in the great past, when he had conquered the hostile dragon, when he had the power of the dragon *with him* in his limbs and breast. When Moses set up the brazen serpent in the wilderness, an act which dominated the imagination of the Jews for many centuries, he was substituting the potency of the good dragon for the sting of the bad dragon, or serpents. That is, man can have the serpent with him or against him. When his serpent is with him, he is almost divine. When his serpent is against him, he is stung and envenomed and defeated from within. The great problem, in the past, was the conquest of the *inimical* serpent and the liberation within the self of the gleaming bright serpent of gold, golden fluid life within the body, the rousing of the splendid divine dragon within a man, or within a woman.

What ails men today is that thousands of little serpents sting and envenom them all the time, and the great divine dragon is inert. We cannot wake him to life, in modern days. He wakes on the lower planes of life: for a while in an airman like Lindbergh or in a boxer like Dempsey. It is the little serpent of gold that lifts these two men for a brief time into a certain level of heroism. But on the higher planes, there is no glimpse or gleam of the great dragon.

The usual vision of the dragon is, however, not personal but cosmic. It is in the vast cosmos of the stars that the dragon writhes and lashes. We see him in his maleficent aspect, red. But don't let us forget that when he stirs green and flashing on a pure dark night of stars it is he who makes the wonder of the night, it is the full rich coiling of his folds which makes the heavens sumptuously serene, as he glides around and guards the immunity, the precious strength of the planets, and gives lustre and new strength to the fixed stars, and still more serene beauty to the moon. His coils within the sun make the sun glad, till the sun dances in radiance. For in his good aspect, the dragon is the great vivifier, the great enhancer of the whole universe.

So he persists still to the Chinese. The long green dragon with which we are so familiar on Chinese things is the dragon in his good aspect of life-bringer, life-giver, life-maker, vivifier. There he coils, on the breasts of the mandarins' coats, looking very horrific, coiling round the centre of the breast and lashing behind with his tail. But as a matter of fact, proud and strong and grand is the mandarin who is within the folds of the green dragon, lord of the dragon.—It is the same dragon which, according to the Hindus, coils quiescent at the base of the spine of a man, and unfolds sometimes lashing along the spinal way: and the yogi is only trying to set this dragon in controlled motion. Dragon-cult is still active and still potent all over the world, particularly in the east.

But alas, the great green dragon of the stars at their brightest is coiled up tight and silent today, in a long winter sleep. Only the red dragon sometimes shows his head, and the millions of little vipers. The millions of little vipers sting us as they stung the murmuring Israelites, and we want some Moses to set the brazen serpent aloft: the serpent which was 'lifted up' even as Jesus later was 'lifted up' for the redemption of men.

The red dragon is the kakodaimon, the dragon in his evil or inimical aspect. In the old lore, red is the colour of *man's* splendour, but the colour of evil in the cosmic creatures or the gods. The red lion is the sun in his evil or destructive aspect. The red dragon is the great 'potency' of the cosmos in its hostile and destructive activity.

The agathodaimon becomes at last the kakodaimon. The green dragon becomes with time the red dragon. What was our joy and our salvation becomes with time, at the end of the time-era, our bane and our damnation. What was a creative god, Ouranos, Kronos, becomes at the end of the time-period a destroyer and a devourer. The god of the beginning of an era is the evil principle at the end of that era. For time still moves in cycles. What was the green dragon, the good potency, at the beginning of the cycle has by the end gradually changed into the red dragon, the evil potency. The good potency of the beginning of the Christian era is now the evil potency of the end.

This is a piece of very old wisdom, and it will always be true. Time still moves in cycles, not in a straight line. And we are at the end of the Christian cycle. And the Logos, the good dragon of the beginning of the cycle, is now the evil dragon of today. It will give its potency to no new thing, only to old and deadly things. It is the red dragon, and it must once more be slain by the heroes, since we can expect no more from the angels.

And, according to old myth, it is woman who falls most absolutely into the power of the dragon, and has no power to escape till man frees her. The new dragon is green or golden, green with the vivid ancient meaning of green which Mohammed took up again, green with that greenish dawn-light which is the quintessence of all new and life-giving light. The dawn of all creation took place in greenish pellucid gleam that was the shine of the very presence of the Creator. John of Patmos harks back to this when he makes the iris or rainbow which screens the face of the Almighty green like smaragd or emerald. And this lovely jewel-green gleam is the very dragon itself, as it moves out wreathing and writhing into the cosmos. It is the power of the Kosmodynamos coiling throughout space, coiling along the spine of a man, leaning forth between his brows like the Uraeus between the brows of a Pharaoh. It makes a man splendid, a king, a hero, a brave man gleaming with the gleam of the dragon, which is golden when it wreathes round a man.

So the Logos came, at the beginning of our era, to give men another sort of splendour. And that same Logos today is the evil snake of the Laocoön which is the death of all of us. The Logos which was like the great green breath of spring-time is now the grey stinging of myriads of deadening little serpents. Now we have to *conquer* the Logos, that the new dragon gleaming green may lean down from among the stars and vivify us and make us great.

And no one is coiled more bitterly in the folds of the old Logos than woman. It is always so. What was a breath of inspiration becomes in the end a fixed and evil *form*, which coils in round like mummy clothes. And then woman is more tightly coiled even than man. Today, the best part of womanhood is wrapped tight and tense in the folds of the Logos, she is bodiless, abstract, and driven by a self-determination terrible to behold. A strange 'spiritual' creature is woman today, driven on and on by the evil demon of the old Logos, never for a moment allowed to escape and be herself. The evil Logos says she must be 'significant', she must 'make something worth while' of her life. So on and on she goes, making something worth while, piling up the evil forms of our civilisation higher and higher, and never for a second escaping to be wrapped in the brilliant fluid folds of the new green dragon. *All* our present life-forms are evil. But with a persistence that would be angelic if it were not devilish woman insists on the *best* in life, by which she means the *best* of our evil life-forms, unable to realise that the best of evil life-forms are the most evil.

So, tragic and tortured by all the grey little snakes of modern shame and pain, she struggles on, fighting for 'the best', which is, alas, the evil best. All women today have a large streak of the policewoman in them. Andromeda was chained naked to a rock, and the dragon of the old form fumed at her. But poor modern Andromeda, she is forced to patrol the streets more or less in policewoman's uniform, with some sort of banner and some sort of bludgeon—or is it called a baton!—up her sleeve, and who is going to rescue her from this? Let her dress up fluffy as she likes, or white and virginal, still underneath it all you can see the stiff folds of the modern policewoman, doing her best, her level best.

Ah God, Andromeda at least had her nakedness, and it was beautiful, and Perseus wanted to fight for her. But our modern policewomen have no nakedness, they have their uniforms. And who could want to fight the dragon of the cold form, the poisonous old Logos, for the sake of a policewoman's uniform?

Ah woman, you have known many bitter experiences. But never, never before have you been condemned by the old dragon to be a policewoman.

O lovely green dragon of the new day, the undawned day, come, come in touch, and release us from the horrid grip of the evil-smelling old Logos! Come in silence, and say nothing. Come in touch, in soft new touch like a spring-time, and say nothing. Come in touch, in soft new touch like a spring-time breeze, and shed these horrible police-woman sheaths from off our women, let the buds of life come nakedly!

In the days of the Apocalypse the old dragon was red. Today he is grey. He was red, because he represented the old way, the old form of power, kingship, riches, ostentation, and lust. By the days of Nero, this old form of ostentation and sensational lust had truly enough become evil, the foul dragon. And the foul dragon, the red one, had to give way to the white dragon of the Logos—Europe with the glorification of white: the white dragon. It ends with the same sanitary worship of white, but the white dragon is now a great white worm, dirty and greyish. Our colour is dirty-white, or grey.

But just as our Logos colour began dazzling white—John of Patmos insists on it, in the white robes of the saints—and ends in a soiled colourlessness, so the old red dragon started marvellously red, glowing golden and blood-red. He was bright, bright, bright red, like the most dazzling vermilion. This, this vivid gold-red was the first colour of the first dragon, far, far back under the very dawn of history. The farthest off men looked at the sky and saw in terms of gold and red, not in terms of green and dazzling white. In terms of gold and red, and the reflection of the dragon in a man's face, in the far-off, far-off past, showed glowing brilliant vermilion. Ah then the heroes and the hero-kings glowed in the face red as poppies that the sun shines through. It was the colour of glory: it was the colour of the wild bright blood, which was life itself. The red, racing bright blood, that was the supreme mystery: the slow, purplish, oozing dark blood, the royal mystery.

The ancient kings of Rome, of the ancient Rome, which was really a thousand years behind the civilisation of the eastern Mediterranean, they painted their faces vermilion, to be divinely royal. And the Red Indians of North America do the same. They are not red save by virtue of this very vermilion paint, which they call 'medicine'. But the Red Indians belong almost to the Neolithic stage of culture, and of religion. Ah, the dark vistas of time in the pueblos of New Mexico, when the men come out with faces glistening scarlet! Gods! they look like gods! It is the red dragon, the beautiful red dragon.

But he became old, and his life-forms became fixed. Even in the pueblos of New Mexico, where the cold life-forms are the life-forms of the great red dragon, the greatest dragon, even there the life-forms are really evil, and the men have a passion for the colour blue, the blue of the turquoise, to escape the red. Turquoise and Silver, these are the colours they yearn for. For gold is of the red dragon. Far-off down the ages gold was the very stuff of the dragon, its soft, gleaming body, prized for the glory of the dragon, and men wore soft gold for glory, like the Aegean and Etruscan warriors in their tombs. And it was not till the red dragon became the kakodaimon, and men began to yearn for the green dragon, and the silver arm-bands, that gold fell from glory and became money. What makes gold into money? the Americans ask you. And there you have it. The death of the great gold dragon, the coming of the green and silver dragon—how the Persians and Babylonians loved turquoise blue, the Chaldeans loved lapis lazuli; so far back they had turned from the red dragon! The dragon of Nebuchadnezzar is blue, and is a blue-scaled unicorn stepping proudly. He is very highly developed. The dragon of the Apocalypse is a much more ancient beast: but then, he is kakodaimon.

But the royal colour still was red: the vermilion and the purple, which is not violet but crimson, the true colour of living blood, these were kept for kings and emperors. They became the very colours of the evil dragon. They are the colours in which the apocalyptist clothes the great harlot woman whom he calls Babylon. The colour of life itself becomes the colour of abomination.

And today, in the day of the dirty-white dragon of the Logos and the Steel Age, the socialists have taken up the oldest of life-colours, and the whole world trembles at a suggestion of vermilion. For the majority today, red is the colour of destruction. 'Red for danger', as the children say. So the cycle goes round: the red and gold dragons of the Gold Age and the Silver Age, the green dragon of the Bronze Age, the white dragon of the Iron Age, the dirty-white dragon, or grey dragon of the Steel Age: and then a return once more to the first brilliant red dragon.

But every heroic epoch turns instinctively to the red dragon, or the gold: every non-heroic epoch instinctively turns away. Like the Apocalypse, where the red and the purple are anathema.

The great red dragon of the Apocalypse had seven heads, each of them crowned: which means his power is royal or supreme in its own manifestation. The seven heads mean he has seven lives, as many lives as a man has natures, or as there are 'potencies' to the cosmos. All his seven heads have to be smitten off, that is, man has another great series of seven conquests to make, this time over the dragon. The fight goes on.

The dragon, being cosmic, destroys a third part of the cosmos before he is cast down out of heaven into earth: he draws down a third part of the stars with his tail. Then the woman brings forth the child who is 'to shepherd mankind with an iron flail'. Alas, if that is a prophecy of the reign of the Messiah, or Jesus, how true it is! For all men today are ruled with a flail of iron. This child is caught up to God: we almost wish the dragon had got him. And the woman fled into the wilderness. That is, the great cosmic mother has no place in the cosmos of men any more. She must hide in the desert since she cannot die.—And there she hides, still during the weary three and a half mystic years which are still going on, apparently.

Now begins the second half of the Apocalypse. We enter the rather boring process of Danielesque prophecy, concerning the Church of Christ and the fall of the various kingdoms of the earth. We cannot be very much interested in the prophesied collapse of Rome and the Roman Empire.

CHAPTER XVII

BUT before we look at this second half, let us glance at the dominant symbols, especially at the symbols of number. The whole scheme is so entirely based on the numbers of seven, four and three, that we may as well try to find out what these numbers meant to the ancient mind.

Three was the sacred number: it is still, for it is the number of the Trinity: it is the number of the nature of God. It is perhaps from the scientists, or the very early philosophers, that we get the most revealing suggestions of the ancient beliefs. The early scientists took the extant religious symbol-ideas and transmuted them into true 'ideas'. We know that the ancients saw number concrete—in dots or in rows of pebbles. And the number three was held by the Pythagoreans to be the perfect number, in their primitive arithmetic, because you could not divide it and leave a gap in the middle. This is obviously true of three pebbles. You cannot destroy the integrity of the three. If you remove one pebble on each side, it still leaves the central stone poised and in perfect balance between the two, like the body of a bird between the two wings. And even as late as the third century, this was felt as the perfect or divine condition of being.

Again, we know that Anaximander, in the fifth century, conceived of the Boundless, the infinite substance, as having its two 'elements', the hot and the cold, the dry and the moist, or fire and the dark, the great 'pair', on either side of it, in the first primordial creation. These three were the beginning of all things. This idea lies at the back of the very ancient division of the *living* cosmos into three, before the idea of God was separated out.

In parenthesis let us remark that the very ancient world was entirely religious and godless. While men still lived in close physical unison, like flocks of birds on the wing, in a close physical oneness, an ancient tribal unison in which

the individual was hardly separated out, then the tribe
lived breast to breast, as it were, with the cosmos, in naked
contact with the cosmos, the whole cosmos was alive and
in contact with the flesh of man, there was no room for
the intrusion of the god idea. It was not till the individual
began to feel separated off, not till he fell into awareness of
himself, and hence into apartness; not, mythologically, till
he ate of the Tree of Knowledge instead of the Tree of
Life, and knew himself *apart* and separate, that the conception of a God arose, to intervene between man and the
cosmos. The very oldest ideas of man are *purely* religious,
and there is no notion of any sort of god or gods. God and
gods enter when man has 'fallen' into a sense of separateness
and loneliness. The oldest philosophers, Anaximander with
his divine Boundless and the divine two elements, and Anaximenes with his divine 'air', are going back to the great
conception of the naked cosmos, before there was God. At
the same time, they know all about the gods of the sixth
century: but they are not strictly interested in them. Even
the first Pythagoreans, who were religious in the conven-
tional way, were more profoundly religious in their conceptions of the two primary forms, Fire and the Night, or Fire
and Dark, dark being conceived of as a kind of thick air or
vapour. These two were the Limit and the Unlimited, Night,
the Unlimited, finding its Limit in Fire. These two primary
forms, being in a tension of opposition, prove their oneness
by their very *opposedness*. Herakleitos says that all things
are an exchange for fire: and that the sun is new every day.
'The limit of dawn and evening is the Bear: and opposite
the Bear is the boundary of bright Zeus.' Bright Zeus is here
supposed to be the bright blue sky, so his boundary is the
horizon, and Herakleitos means probably that opposite the
Bear, that is down, down in the antipodes, it is always
night, and Night lives the death of Day, as Day lives the
death of Night.

This is the state of mind of great men in the fifth and
fourth centuries before Christ, strange and fascinating and
a revelation of the old symbolic mind. Religion was already
turning moralistic or ecstatic, with the Orphics the tedious
idea of 'escaping the wheel of birth' had begun to abstract
men from life. But early science is a source of the purest
and oldest religion. The mind of man recoiled, there in

Ionia, to the oldest religious conception of the cosmos, from which to start thinking out the scientific cosmos. And the thing the oldest philosophers disliked was the new sort of religious conception, with its ecstasies and its escape and its purely *personal* nature: its loss of the cosmos.

So the first philosophers took up the sacred three-part cosmos of the ancients. It is paralleled in Genesis, where we have a god creation, in the division into heaven, and earth, and water: the first three *created* elements, presupposing a God who creates. The ancient threefold division of the living heavens, the Chaldean, is made when the heavens themselves are divine, and not merely God-inhabited. Before men felt any need of God or gods, while the vast heavens lived of themselves and lived breast to breast with man, the Chaldeans gazed up in religious rapture. And then by some strange intuition, they divided the heavens into three sections. And then they really *knew* the stars as the stars have never been known since.

Later, when a God or Maker or Ruler of the skies was invented or discovered, then the heavens were divided into the four quarters, the old four quarters that lasted so long. And then, gradually with the invention of a God or a Demiurge, the old star-knowledge and true worship declined with the Babylonians into magic and astrology, the whole system was 'worked'. But still the old Chaldean cosmic knowledge persisted, and this the Ionians must have picked up again.

Even during the four-quarter centuries, the heavens still had three primary rulers, sun, moon, and morning-star. But the Bible says, sun, moon, and stars.

The morning-star was always a god, from the time when gods began. But when the cult of dying and reborn gods started all over the old world, about 600 B.C., he became symbolic of the new god, because he rules in the twilight, between day and night, and for the same reason he is supposed to be lord of both, and to stand gleaming with one foot on the flood of night and one foot on the world of day, one foot on sea and one on shore. We know that night was a form of vapour or flood.

CHAPTER XVIII

THREE is the number of things divine, and four is the number of creation. The world is four-square, divided into four quarters which are ruled by four great creatures, the four winged creatures that surround the throne of the Almighty. These four great creatures make up the sum of mighty space, both dark and light, and their wings are the quivering of this space, that trembles all the time with thunderous praise of the Creator: for these are Creation praising their Maker, as Creation shall praise its Maker forever. That their wings (strictly) are full of eyes before and behind, only means that they are the stars of the trembling heavens forever changing and travelling and pulsing. In Ezekiel, muddled and mutilated as the text is, we see the four great creatures amid the wheels of the revolving heavens—a conception which belongs to the seventh, sixth, and fifth centuries— and supporting on their wing-tips the crystal vault of the final heaven of the throne.

In their origin, the Creatures are probably older than God himself. They were a very grand conception, and some suggestion of them is at the back of most of the great winged Creatures of the east. They belong to the last age of the living cosmos, the cosmos that was not created, that had yet no god in it because it was in itself utterly divine and primal. Away behind all the creation myths lies the grand idea that the cosmos *always was*, that it could not have had any beginning, because it always was there and always would be there. It could not have a god to start it, because it was itself all god and all divine, the origin of everything.

This living cosmos man first divided into three parts: and then, at some point of great change, we cannot know when, he divided it instead into four quarters, and the four quarters demanded a whole, a conception of the whole, and then a maker, a Creator. So the four great elemental creatures became subordinate, they surrounded the supreme central unit, and their wings cover all space. Later still, they are turned from vast and living elements into beasts or Creatures or Cherubim—it is a process of degradation—and given the four elemental or cosmic natures of man, lion, bull, and eagle. In Ezekiel, each of the creatures is all four at once, with a different face looking in each direction. But in the Apocalypse each beast has its own face. And as the cosmic idea dwindled, we get the four cosmic natures of the four Creatures applied first to the great Cherubim then to the personified Archangels, Michael, Gabriel, etc., and finally they are applied to the four Evangelists, Matthew, Mark, Luke, and John. 'Four for the Gospel Natures.' It is all a process of degradation or personification of a great old concept.

Parallel to the division of the cosmos into four quarters, four parts, and four dynamic 'natures' comes the other division, into four elements. At first, it seems as if there had been only three elements: heaven, earth, and sea, or water: heaven being primarily light or fire. The recognition of air came later. But with the elements of fire, earth, and water the cosmos was complete, air being conceived of as a form of vapour, darkness the same.

And the earliest scientists (philosophers) seemed to want to make one element, or at most two, responsible for the cosmos. Anaximenes said all was water. Xenophanes said all was earth and water. Water gave off moist exhalations, and in these moist exhalations were latent sparks; these exhalations blew aloft as clouds, they blew far, aloft, and condensed *upon their sparks* instead of into water, and thus they produced stars: thus they even produced the sun. The sun was a great 'cloud' of assembled sparks from the moist exhalations of the watery earth. This is how science began: far more fantastic than myth, but using processes of reason.

Then came Herakleitos with his: All is Fire, or rather: All is an exchange for Fire, and his insistence on Strife, which holds things asunder and so holds them integral and makes their existence even possible, as the creative *principle*: Fire being an element.

After which the Four Elements become almost inevitable. With Empedokles in the fifth century the Four Elements of Fire, Earth, Air, and Water established themselves in the imagination of men forever, the four *living* or cosmic elements, the radical elements: the Four Roots Empedokles called them, the four cosmic roots of all existence. And they were controlled by two principles, Love and Strife.— 'Fire and Water and Earth and the mighty height of Air; dread Strife, too, apart from these, of equal weight to each, and Love in their midst, equal in length and breadth.' And again Empedokles calls the Four: 'shining Zeus, life-bringing Hera, Aidoneus, and Vestis.' So we see the Four also as gods: the Big Four of the ages. When we consider the four elements, we shall see that they are, now and forever, the four elements of our experience. All that science has taught about fire does not make fire any different. The processes of combustion are not fire, they are thought-forms. H_2O is not water, it is a thought-form derived from experiments with water. Thought-forms are thought-forms, they do not make our life. Our life is made still of elemental fire and water, earth and air: by these we move and live and have our being.

From the four elements we come to the four natures of man himself, based on the conception of blood, bile, lymph, and phlegm, and their properties. Man is still a creature that thinks with his blood: 'the heart, dwelling in the sea of blood that runs in opposite directions, where chiefly is what men call thought; for the blood round the heart is the thought of men'.—And maybe this is true. Maybe all basic thought takes place in the blood around the heart, and is only transferred to the brain. Then there are the Four Ages, based on the four metals: gold, silver, bronze, and iron. In the sixth century already the Iron Age had set in, and already man laments it. The age before the eating of the Fruit of Knowledge is left far behind.

The first scientists, then, are very near to the old symbolists. And so we see in the Apocalypse, that when St. John is referring to the old primal or divine cosmos, he speaks of a third part of this, that, or another: as when the dragon, who belongs to the old divine cosmos, draws down a third part of the stars with his tail: or where the divine trumps destroy a third part of things: or the horsemen from the abyss, which are divine demons, destroy a third part of man. But when the destruction is by non-divine agency, it is usually a fourth part that is destroyed. —Anyhow there is far too much destroying in the Apocalypse. It ceases to be fun.

CHAPTER XIX

THE numbers four and three together make up the sacred number seven: the cosmos with its god. The Pythagoreans called it 'the number of the right time'. Man and the cosmos alike have four created natures, and three divine natures. Man has his four earthly natures, then soul, spirit, and the eternal I. The universe has the four quarters and the four elements, then also the three divine quarters of Heaven, Hades, and the Whole, and the three divine motions of Love, Strife, and Wholeness.—The oldest cosmos had not Heaven nor Hades. But then it is probable that seven is not a sacred number in the oldest consciousness of man.

It is always, from the beginning, however, a semi-sacred number because it is the number of the seven ancient planets, which began with the sun and moon, and included the five great 'wandering' stars, Jupiter, Venus, Mercury, Mars, and Saturn. The wandering planets were always a great mystery to man, especially in the days when he lived breast to breast with the cosmos, and watched the moving heavens with a profundity of passionate attention quite different from any form of attention today.

The Chaldeans always preserved some of the elemental immediacy of the cosmos, even to the end of Babylonian days. They had, later, their whole mythology of Marduk and the rest, and the whole bag of tricks of their astrologers and magi, but it never seems to have ousted, entirely, the direct star-lore, nor to have broken altogether the breast to breast contact of the star-gazer and the skies of night. The magi continued, apparently, through the ages concerned only in the mysteries of the heavens, without any god or gods dragged in. That the heaven-lore degenerated into tedious forms of divination and magic later on is only part of human history: everything human degenerates, from religion downwards, and must be renewed and revived.

It was this preserving of star-lore naked and without gods that prepared the way for astronomy later, just as in the eastern Mediterranean a great deal of old cosmic lore about water and fire must have lingered and prepared the way for the Ionian philosophers and modern science.

The great control of the life of earth from the living and intertwining heavens was an idea which had far greater hold of the minds of men before the Christian era than we realise. In spite of all the gods and goddesses, the Jehovah and the dying and redeeming Saviours of many nations, underneath the old cosmic vision remained, and men believed, perhaps, more radically in the rule of the stars than in any of the gods. Man's consciousness has many layers, and the lowest layers continue to be crudely active, especially down among the common people, for centuries after the cultured consciousness of the nation has passed to higher planes. And the consciousness of man always tends to revert to the original levels; though there are two modes of reversion: by degeneration and decadence; and by deliberate return in order to get back to the roots again, for a new start.

In Roman times there was a great slipping back of the human consciousness to the oldest levels, though it was a form of decadence and a return to superstition. But in the first two centuries after Christ the rule of the heavens returned on man as never before, with a power of superstition stronger than any religious cult. Horoscopy was the rage. Fate, fortune, destiny, character, everything depended on the stars, which meant, on the seven planets. The seven planets were the seven Rulers of the heavens, and they fixed the fate of man irrevocably, inevitably. Their rule became at last a form of insanity, and both the Christians and the Neo-Platonists set their faces against it.

Now this element of superstition bordering on magic and occultism is very strong in the Apocalypse. The Revelation of John is, we must admit it, a book to conjure with. It is full of suggestions for occult use, and it has been used, throughout the ages, for occult purposes, for the purpose of divination and prophecy especially. It lends itself to this. Nay, the book is written, especially the second half, in a spirit of lurid prophecy very like the magical utterances of the occultists of the time. It reflects the spirit of the time:

as *The Golden Ass* reflects that of less than a hundred years later, not very different.

So that the number seven ceases almost to be the 'divine' number, and becomes the magical number of the Apocalypse. As the book proceeds, the ancient divine element fades out and the 'modern', first century taint of magic, prognostication, and occult practice takes its place. Seven is the number now of divination and conjuring rather than of real vision.

So the famous 'time, times and a half', which means three and a half years. It comes from Daniel who already starts the semi-occult business of prophesying the fall of empires. It is supposed to represent the half of a sacred week—all that is ever allowed to the princes of evil, who are never given the full run of the sacred week of seven 'days'. But with John of Patmos it is a magic number.

In the old days, when the moon was a great power in heaven, ruling men's bodies and swaying the flux of the flesh, then seven was one of the moon's quarters. The moon still sways the flux of the flesh, and still we have a seven-day week. The Greeks of the sea had a nine-day week. That is gone.

But the number seven is no longer divine. Perhaps it is still to some extent magical.

CHAPTER XX

THE number ten is the natural number of a series. 'It is by nature that the Hellenes count up to ten and then start over again.' It is of course the number of the fingers of the two hands. This repetition of five observed throughout nature was one of the things that led the Pythagoreans to assert that 'all things are number'. In the Apocalypse, ten is the 'natural' or complete number of a series. The Pythagoreans, experimenting with pebbles, found that ten pebbles could be laid out in a triangle of $4+3+2+1$: and this sent their minds off in imagination.—But the ten heads or crowned horns of John's two evil beasts probably represent merely a complete series of emperors or kings, horn being a stock symbol for empires or their rulers. The old symbol of horns, of course, is the symbol of power, originally the divine power that came to man from the vivid cosmos, from the starry green dragon of life, but especially from the vivid dragon within the body, that lies coiled at the base of the spine, and flings himself sometimes along the spinal way till he flushes the brow with magnificence, the gold horns of power that bud on Moses' forehead, or the gold serpent, Uraeus, which came down between the brows of the royal Pharaohs of Egypt, and is the dragon of the individual. But for the commonalty, the horn of power was the ithyphallos, the phallos, the cornucopia.

CHAPTER XXI

THE final number, twelve, is the number of the established or unchanging cosmos, as contrasted with the seven of the wandering planets, which are the physical (in the old Greek sense) cosmos, always in motion apart from the rest of motion. Twelve is the number of the signs of the zodiac, and of the months of the year. It is three times four, or four times three: the complete correspondence. It is the whole round of the heavens, and the whole round of man. For man had seven natures in the old scheme: that is, $6 + 1$, the last being the nature of his wholeness. But now he has quite another new nature, as well as the old one: for we admit he still is made up of the old Adam *plus* the new. So now his number is twelve, $6 + 6$ for his natures, and one for his wholeness. But his wholeness is now in Christ: no longer symbolised between his brows. And now that his number is twelve, man is perfectly rounded and established, established and unchanging, for he is now perfect and there is no need for him to change, his wholeness, which is his thirteenth number (unlucky in superstition), being with Christ in heaven. Such was the opinion of the 'saved', concerning themselves. Such is still the orthodox opinion: those that are saved in Christ are perfect and unchanging, no need for them to change. They are perfectly individualised.

CHAPTER XXII

WHEN we come to the second half of Revelation, after the new-born child is snatched to heaven and the woman has fled into the wilderness, there is a sudden change, and we feel we are reading purely Jewish and Jewish-Christian Apocalypse, with none of the old background.

'And there was war in heaven: Michael and his angels fought against the dragon.' They cast down the dragon out of heaven into the earth, and he becomes Satan, and ceases entirely to be interesting. When the great figures of mythology are turned into rationalised or merely moral forces, then they lose interest. We are acutely bored by moral angels and moral devils. We are acutely bored by a 'rationalised' Aphrodite. Soon after 1000 B.C. the world went a little insane about morals and 'sin'. The Jews had always been tainted.

What we have been looking for in the Apocalypse is something older, grander than the ethical business. The old, flaming love of life and the strange shudder of the presence of the invisible dead made the rhythm of really ancient religion. Moral religion is comparatively modern, even with the Jews.

But the second half of the Apocalypse is all moral: that is to say, it is all sin and salvation. For a moment there is a hint of the old cosmic wonder, when the dragon turns again upon the woman and she is given wings of an eagle and flies off into the wilderness: but the dragon pursues her and spues out a flood upon her, to overwhelm her: 'And the earth helped the woman, and the earth opened her mouth, and swallowed up the flood. . . . And the dragon was wroth with the woman, and went to make war with the remnant of her seed, *which keep the commandments of God, and have the testimony of Jesus Christ.*'

The last words are, of course, the moral ending tacked on

by some Jew-Christian scribe to the fragment of myth. The
dragon is here the watery dragon, or the dragon of chaos,
and in his evil aspect still. He is resisting with all his might
the birth of a new thing, or new era. He turns against the
Christians, since they are the only 'good' thing left on
earth.

The poor dragon henceforth cuts a sorry figure. He gives
his power, and his seat, and great authority to the beast
that rises out of the sea, the beast with 'seven heads and
ten horns, and upon his horns ten crowns and upon his
heads the name of blasphemy. And the beast which I saw
was like unto a leopard, and his feet were as the feet of a
bear, and his mouth as the mouth of a lion.'

We know this beast already: he comes out of Daniel and
is *explained* by Daniel. The beast is the last grand world-
empire, the ten horns are ten kingdoms confederated in the
empire—which is of course Rome. As for the leopard, bear,
and lion qualities, these are also explained in Daniel as the
three empires that preceded Rome, the Macedonian, swift as
a leopard, the Persian, stubborn as a bear, the Babylonians,
rapacious as the lion.

We are back again at the level of allegory, and for me,
the real interest is gone. Allegory can always be explained:
and explained away. The true symbol defies all explanation,
so does the true myth. You can give meanings to either—
you will never explain them away. Because symbol and
myth do not affect us only mentally, they move the deep
emotional centres every time. The great quality of the
mind is finality. The mind 'understands', and there's an end
of it.

But the emotional consciousness of man has a life and
movement quite different from the mental consciousness.
The mind knows in part, in part and parcel, with full stop
after every sentence. But the emotional soul knows in full,
like a river or a flood. For example, the symbol of the dragon
—look at it, on a Chinese tea-cup or in an old wood-cut,
read it in a fairy-tale—and what is the result? If you are
alive in the old emotional self, the more you look at the
dragon, and think of it, the farther and farther flushes out
your emotional awareness, on and on into dim regions of
the soul aeons and aeons back. But if you are dead in the
old feeling-knowing way, as so many moderns are, then

the dragon just 'stands for' this, that, and the other—all the
things it stands for in Frazer's *Golden Bough*: it is just a
kind of glyph or label, like the gilt pestle and mortar outside
a chemist's shop. Or take better still the Egyptian symbol
called the *ankh*, the symbol of life, etc., which the goddesses
hold in their hands. Any child 'knows what it means'. But
a man who is *really* alive feels his soul begin to throb and
expand at the mere sight of the symbol. Modern men, however, are nearly all half dead, modern women too. So they
just look at the *ankh* and know all about it, and that's that.
They are proud of their own emotional impotence.

Naturally, then, the Apocalypse has appealed to men
through the ages as an 'allegorical' work. Everything just
'meant something' and something moral at that. You can put
down the meaning flat—plain as two and two make four.

The beast from the sea means Roman Empire—and later
Nero, number 666. The beast from the earth means the
pagan sacerdotal power, the priestly power which made the
emperors divine and made Christians even 'worship' them.
For the beast from the earth has two horns, like a lamb,
a false Lamb indeed, an Antichrist, and it teaches its wicked
followers to perform marvels and even miracles—of witch-
craft, like Simon Magus and the rest.

So we have the Church of Christ—or of the Messiah—
being martyred by the beast, till pretty well all good Christians are martyred. Then at last, after not so very long a
time—say forty years—the Messiah descends from heaven
and makes war on the beast, the Roman Empire, and on the
kings who are with him. There is a grand fall of Rome,
called Babylon, and a grand triumph over her downfall—
though the best poetry is all the time lifted from Jeremiah or
Ezekiel or Isaiah, it is not original. The sainted Christians
gloat over fallen Rome: and then the Victorious Rider
appears, his shirt bloody with the blood of dead kings. After
this, a New Jerusalem descends to be his Bride, and these
precious martyrs all get their thrones, and for a thousand
years (John was not going to be put off with Enoch's
meagre forty), for a thousand years, the grand Millennium,
the Lamb reigns over the earth, assisted by all the risen
martyrs. And if the martyrs in the Millennium are going to be
as bloodthirsty and ferocious as John the Divine in the
Apocalypse—Revenge! Timotheus cries—then somebody's

going to get it hot during the thousand years of the rule
of Saints.

But this is not enough. After the thousand years the
whole universe must be wiped out, earth, sun, moon, stars,
and sea. These early Christians fairly lusted after the end
of the world. They wanted their own grand turn first—
Revenge! Timotheus cries.—But after that, they insisted that
the whole universe must be wiped out, sun, stars, and all—
and a *new* New Jerusalem should appear, with the same old
saints and martyrs in glory, and everything else should
have disappeared except the lake of burning brimstone in
which devils, demons, beasts and bad men should frizzle
and suffer for ever and ever and ever, Amen!

So ends this glorious work: surely a rather repulsive work.
Revenge was indeed a sacred duty to the Jerusalem Jews:
and it is not the revenge one minds so much as the perpetual
self-glorification of these saints and martyrs, and their profound impudence. How one loathes them, in their 'new
white garments'. How disgusting their priggish rule must be!
How vile is their spirit, really, insisting, simply insisting on
wiping out the whole universe, bird and blossom, star and
river, and above all, everybody except *themselves* and their
precious 'saved' brothers. How beastly their New Jerusalem,
where the flowers never fade, but stand in everlasting same-
ness! How terribly bourgeois to have unfading flowers!

No wonder the pagans were horrified at the 'impious'
Christian desire to destroy the universe. How horrified even
the old Jews of the Old Testament would have been! For
even to them, earth and sun and stars were eternal, created
in the grand creation by Almighty God. But no, these im-
pudent martyrs must see it all go up in smoke.

Oh, it is the Christianity of the middling masses, this
Christianity of the Apocalypse. And we must confess, it is
hideous. Self-righteousness, self-conceit, self-importance and
secret *envy* underlie it all.

By the time of Jesus, all the lowest classes and mediocre
people had realised that *never* would they get a chance to
be kings, *never* would they go in chariots, never would they
drink wine from gold vessels. Very well then—they would
have their revenge by *destroying* it all. 'Babylon the great
is fallen, is fallen, and is become the habitation of devils.'
And then all the gold and silver and pearls and precious

stones and fine linen and purple, and silk, and scarlet—and cinnamon and frankincense, wheat, beasts, sheep, horses, chariots, slaves, souls of men—all these that are destroyed, destroyed, destroyed in Babylon the great—how one hears the envy, the endless envy screeching through this song of triumph!

No, we can understand that the Fathers of the Church in the east wanted Apocalypse left out of the New Testament. And like Judas among the disciples, it was inevitable that it should be included. The Apocalypse is the feet of clay to the grand Christian image. And down crashes the image, on the weakness of these very feet.

There is Jesus—but there is also John the Divine. There is Christian love—and there is Christian envy. The former would 'save' the world—the latter will never be satisfied till it has destroyed the world. They are two sides of the same medal.

CHAPTER XXIII

BECAUSE, as a matter of fact, when you start to teach individual self-realisation to the great masses of people, who when all is said and done are only *fragmentary* beings, *incapable* of whole individuality, you end by making them all envious, grudging, spiteful creatures. Anyone who is kind to man knows the fragmentariness of most men, and wants to arrange a society of power in which men fall naturally into a collective wholeness, since they *cannot* have an individual wholeness. In this collective wholeness they will be fulfilled. But if they make efforts at individual fulfilment, they *must fail* for they are by nature fragmentary. Then, failures, having no wholeness anywhere, they fall into envy and spite. Jesus knew all about it when he said: To them that have shall be given, etc. But he had forgotten to reckon with the mass of the mediocre, whose motto is: We have nothing and therefore nobody shall have anything.

But Jesus gave the ideal for the Christian individual, and deliberately avoided giving an ideal for the State or the nation. When he said, 'Render unto Caesar that which is Caesar's', he left to Caesar the rule of men's bodies, willy-nilly: and this threatened terrible danger to a man's mind and soul. Already by the year A.D. 60 the Christians were an accursed sect; and they were compelled, like all men, to sacrifice, that is to give worship to the living Caesar. In giving Caesar the power over men's bodies, Jesus gave him the power to compel men to make the act of worship to Caesar. Now I doubt if Jesus himself could have performed this act of worship, to a Nero or a Domitian. No doubt he would have preferred death. As did so many early Christian martyrs. So there, at the very beginning was a monstrous dilemma. To be a Christian meant death at the hands of the Roman State; for refusal to submit to the cult of the

Emperor and worship the divine man, Caesar, was impossible to a Christian. No wonder, then, that John of Patmos saw the day not far off when *every* Christian would be martyred. The day would have come, if the imperial cult had been absolutely enforced on the people. And then when *every* Christian was martyred, what could a Christian expect but a Second Advent, resurrection, and an absolute revenge! There was a condition for the Christian community to be in, sixty years after the death of the Saviour.

Jesus made it inevitable, when he said that the money belonged to Caesar. It was a mistake. Money means bread, and the bread of men belongs to no men. Money means also power, and it is monstrous to give power to the virtual enemy. Caesar was *bound*, sooner or later, to violate the soul of the Christians. But Jesus saw the individual only, and considered only the individual. He left it to John of Patmos, who was up against the Roman State, to formulate the Christian vision of the Christian State. John did it in the Apocalypse. It entails the destruction of the whole world, and the reign of saints in ultimate bodiless glory. Or it entails the destruction of all earthly power, and the rule of an oligarchy of martyrs (the Millennium).

This destruction of all earthly power we are now moving towards. The oligarchy of martyrs began with Lenin, and apparently others also are martyrs. Strange, strange people they are, the martyrs, with weird, cold morality. When every country has its martyr-ruler, either like Lenin or like those, what a strange, unthinkable world it will be! But it is coming: the Apocalypse is still a book to conjure with.

A few vastly important points have been missed by Christian doctrine and Christian thought. Christian fantasy alone has grasped them.

1. No man is or can be a pure individual. The mass of men have only the tiniest touch of individuality: if any. The mass of men live and move, think and feel collectively, and have practically no individual emotions, feelings or thoughts at all. They are fragments of the collective or social consciousness. It has always been so. And will always be so.

2. The State, or what we call Society as a collective whole *cannot* have the psychology of an individual. Also it is a mistake to say that the State is made up of individuals.

It is not. It is made up of a collection of fragmentary beings. And *no* collective act, even so private an act as voting, is made from the individual self. It is made from the collective self, and has another psychological background, non-individual.

3. The State *cannot* be Christian. Every State is a Power. It cannot be otherwise. Every State must guard its own boundaries and guard its own prosperity. If it fails to do so, it betrays all its individual citizens.

4. Every *citizen* is a unit of worldly power. A *man* may wish to be a pure Christian and a pure individual. But since he *must* be a member of some political State, or nation, he is forced to be a unit of worldly power.

5. As a citizen, as a collective being, man has his fulfilment in the gratification of his power-sense. If he belongs to one of the so-called 'ruling nations', his soul is fulfilled in the sense of his country's power or strength. If his country mounts up aristocratically to a zenith of splendour and power, in a hierarchy, he will be all the more fulfilled, having his place in the hierarchy. But if his country is powerful and democratic, then he will be obsessed with a perpetual will to assert his power in interfering and *preventing* other people from doing as they wish, since no man must do more than another man. This is the condition of modern democracies, a condition of perpetual bullying.

In democracy, bullying inevitably takes the place of power. Bullying is the negative form of power. The modern Christian State is a soul-destroying force, for it is made up of fragments which have no organic whole, only a collective whole. In a hierarchy each part is organic and vital, as my finger is an organic and vital part of me. But a democracy is bound in the end to be obscene, for it is composed of myriad disunited fragments, each fragment assuming to itself a false wholeness, a false individuality. Modern democracy is made up of millions of frictional parts all asserting their own wholeness.

6. To have an ideal for the individual which regards only his individual self and ignores his collective self is in the long run fatal. To have a creed of individuality which denies the reality of the hierarchy makes at last for more anarchy. Democratic man lives by cohesion and resistance, the cohesive force of 'love' and the resistant force of the individual

'freedom'. To yield entirely to love would be to be absorbed, which is the death of the individual: for the individual must hold his own, or he ceases to be 'free' and individual. So that we see, what our age has proved to its astonishment and dismay, that the individual *cannot* love. The individual cannot love: let that be an axiom. And the modern man or woman *cannot* conceive of himself, herself, save as an individual. And the individual in man or woman is *bound* to kill, at last, the lover in himself or herself. It is not that each man kills the thing he loves, but that each man, by insisting on his own individuality, kills the lover in himself, as the woman kills the lover in herself. The Christian *dare not love*: for love kills that which is Christian, democratic, and modern, the individual. The individual *cannot* love. When the individual loves, he ceases to be purely individual. And so he *must* recover himself, and cease to love. It is one of the most amazing lessons of our day: that the individual, the Christian, the democrat *cannot* love. Or, when he loves, when she loves, he *must* take it back, she *must* take it back.

So much for private or personal love. Then what about that other love, 'caritas', loving your neighbour as yourself?

It works out the same. You love your neighbour. Immediately you run the risk of being absorbed by him: you must draw back, you must hold your own. The love becomes resistance. In the end, it is all resistance and no love: which is the history of democracy.

If you are taking the path of individual self-realisation, you had better, like Buddha, go off and be by yourself, and give a thought to nobody. Then you may achieve your Nirvana. Christ's way of loving your neighbour leads to the hideous anomaly of having to live by sheer resistance to your neighbour, in the end.

The Apocalypse, strange book, makes this clear. It shows us the Christian in his relation to the State; which the gospels and epistles avoid doing. It shows us the Christian in relation to the State, to the world, and to the cosmos. It shows him in mad hostility to all of them, having, in the end, to will the destruction of them all.

It is the dark side of Christianity, of individualism, and of democracy, the side the world at large now shows us. And it is, simply, suicide. Suicide individual and *en masse*.

If man could will it, it would be cosmic suicide. But the cosmos is not at man's mercy, and the sun will not perish to please us.

We do not want to perish, either. We have to give up a false position. Let us give up our false position as Christians, as individuals, as democrats. Let us find some conception of ourselves that will allow us to be peaceful and happy, instead of tormented and unhappy.

The Apocalypse shows us what we are resisting, unnaturally. We are unnaturally resisting our connection with the cosmos, with the world, with mankind, with the nation, with the family. All these connections are, in the Apocalypse, anathema, and they are anathema to us. We *cannot bear connection*. That is our malady. We *must* break away, and be isolate. We call that being free, being individual. Beyond a certain point, which we have reached, it is suicide. Perhaps we have chosen suicide. Well and good. The Apocalypse too chose suicide, with subsequent self-glorification.

But the Apocalypse shows us, by its very resistance, the things that the human heart secretly yearns after. By the very frenzy with which the Apocalypse destroys the sun and the stars, the world, and all kings and all rulers, all scarlet and purple and cinnamon, all harlots, finally all men altogether who are not 'sealed', we can see how deeply the apocalyptists are yearning for the sun and the stars and the earth and the waters of the earth, for nobility and lordship and might, and scarlet and gold splendour, for passionate love, and a proper unison with men, apart from this sealing business. What man most passionately wants is his living wholeness and his living unison, not his own isolate salvation of his 'soul'. Man wants his physical fulfilment first and foremost, since now, once and once only, he is in the flesh and potent. For man, the vast marvel is to be alive. For man, as for flower and beast and bird, the supreme triumph is to be most vividly, most perfectly alive. Whatever the unborn and the dead may know, they cannot know the beauty, the marvel of being alive in the flesh. The dead may look after the afterwards. But the magnificent here and now of life in the flesh is ours, and ours alone, and ours only for a time. We ought to dance with rapture that we should be alive and in the flesh, and part of the living, incarnate cosmos. I am part of the sun as my eye is part of me. That I am part of the earth my feet know perfectly, and my blood is part of the sea. My soul knows that I am part of the human race, my soul is an organic part of the great human soul, as my spirit is part of my nation. In my own very self, I am part of my family. There is nothing of me that is alone and absolute except my mind, and we shall find that the mind has no existence by itself, it is only the glitter of the sun on the surface of the waters.

So that my individualism is really an illusion. I am a part of the great whole, and I can never escape. But I *can* deny my connections, break them, and become a fragment. Then I am wretched.

What we want is to destroy our false, inorganic connections, especially those related to money, and re-establish the living organic connections, with the cosmos, the sun and earth, with mankind and nation and family. Start with the sun, and the rest will slowly, slowly happen.

Jan Maarten

T. DE VRIES-KRUYT

Small Ship
Great Sea

the life story of a mongoloid boy

translated from the Dutch by
Vivienne van Kretschmar

photographs by Cas Oorthuys
and others

Collins
London & Glasgow

ISBN 0 00 460201 3

First published by Uitgeverij Contact Amsterdam 1966
This edition in English first published 1971
© Copyright Dutch edition Contact-Amsterdam 1966
© This translation copyright T. de Vries-Kruyt 1971

Printed in Great Britain   Collins Clear-Type Press

PROLOGUE

The restaurant at Oostergo looked particularly
cheerful that day. The sun did its best outside,
and its rays were reflected into the room by the
water, so that the light shimmering on the walls
and over the tables created the impression that it
was on board ship. It was an ideal spot for a
celebration, and that was what the people at the
centre table were doing.
The six girls were enjoying dinner with the
middle-aged couple who had come over for the
evening with their son to the sailing resort, where
the girls were spending a holiday.
The table was noisy with stories about the school
certificate examinations they had just sat, and
there was also a more recent incident involving a
broken mast. That they were all relaxed and happy
was evident to the rest of the room, and it wasn't
surprising that some of the other guests eaves-
dropped every now and then. The host was teasing
the girls, who had obviously steered more sucess-
fully through school exams than over the local
lake. As usual, the members of the crew could
not agree on the cause of the accident.
'What do you think, Jan Maarten?' they asked the
boy.

'No comment. I'm only an "O" level type.'

There was a moment's silence before they all shouted with laughter at this unexpected reply.

Jan Maarten sat looking very pleased with himself. His father and mother were at either end of the table. Shortly afterwards the waiter asked the father if he would mind having a word with a couple sitting near the window. Of course not. As he approached the two strangers he wondered if he should know them. Was she an ex-pupil of his? (He had taught in Amsterdam during the war.) Or was the husband a business contact he did not at once recognize?

'You don't know us and we don't know you, but we have a boy just like your son. How is it that he is so "normal"?'

Jan Maarten de Vries is a backward child of the type known as 'mongoloid'. He is now in his twenties. As to his health, he is an exceptionally fragile craft to keep afloat, but he is a brave boy who often makes severer demands on himself than a healthy, normal person would. He is polite, happy, has a sense of humour and a well-developed sense of duty, he is always busy and is a very dear member of the family.

'How is it that your son is so "normal"?'

It is not the first time we have been asked that question. Acquaintances who come to us for advice about their backward children ask it too. The paediatrician who treated him for diabetes put it almost impatiently, imperatively.

6

'Your son is an average case of mongolism,' he added. 'I've known others who were much more intelligent but who have remained far more retarded. How did you stimulate his development to this extent?'

There are many children like Jan Maarten, as a visit to any school for the retarded will demonstrate. Many children are born suffering from mongolism . . . And when I try to answer that question, usually asked with such a world of emotion behind it, I always think of the very young ones who still have a future before them, who still have it in them to become either a blessing or an intolerable burden.

If we answered in general terms, we would have to admit that we were lucky. We had learned to accept our griefs before he was a year old and were busy finding out how best we could bring him up. That was in 1941. Neither of our families had ever been confronted with an abnormal child before. The war reduced our sorrow to the proper proportions, and in those times it was a privilege to grieve over something that had not been brought about by others. There are a number of doctors in our family and many of our friends are doctors too. Not one of them has ever been reluctant to give us advice. This has saved the boy's life time and again. These children are delicate and often react to normal illnesses so unexpectedly that only quick action can save them.

7

Another point in our favour was that Jan Maarten was our eldest child. It was therefore not necessary for us to alter an established pattern, geared to the needs of normal children. We had time to think about how we would solve various problems, and we took the trouble to note our mistakes and to set them right.

Yes, Jan Maarten, we were very lucky.

It is to help others find the happiness that can rise out of great sorrow that I shall try to answer the question 'How is it that Jan Maarten is what he is?' In order to do so, I shall explore the submerged storehouse of my memories, which is something we all love to do at different times and in different moods. I once had the privilege, when skin-diving in Biak, of seeing the silent golden world past the coral reef, a fascinating world full of colours, light and dark. It is difficult to say exactly what I saw, since that depended largely on the angle at which the rays of the sun struck the water.

When I examine that brightly coloured fish, Jan Maarten, in the deep-sea world of my memory, I try to find the right light that will illumine some moments in his life that may be of interest to others. Who are those others? They are all those parents with whom we feel a close bond, who want to do their best for the child who is different from the others. First he is everybody's plaything, everybody's darling, until almost imperceptibly he becomes a problem, a tyrant in

8

his doubts. It would not have been fair to have pretended at a time like this.

The father had found an ally, and together they watched the changes and developments in the child as the months went by. The mother loved the baby completely and utterly.

'You're not beautiful, but you're all mine.'

The first baby is an experience that is not easily described. This tiny, living thing in your arms depends on you wholly. Cherish it, whisper endearments while you hug its warmth to the warmth of your body – it is yours as nothing ever has been, ever before. Time stands still. Is there a future full of problems? Of course not. There is a cot with a child close by, eyes that watch you as the tiny mouth drinks. You, baby, you are the whole world to your mother and father.

The mother was able to hide behind the barricade of her joy in the child as a child and of her daily care of him. Her mind registered the deviations but immediately postponed judgement. A doctor does not like to commit himself before the child's first birthday, she thought. A year, a whole year! The front door of the little house opened on the outside world and the outside world was at war.

When father and mother said goodbye to each other every morning, they did not hurry their farewells for every parting could have been for a long, long time. How much could happen in a year! And in all that time the child was with them, was theirs.

11

The father's fears broke like a wave on the rock of the mother's happiness. He could not go on as if everything was normal, he could not be glad about something that was sure to bring unhappiness. And he was sure that the future could not be happy. A man and a woman, travelling the same *via dolorosa*, will react differently to their sorrows. But they should share them; it is not good to travel alone.

When Jan Maarten was eight months old, his father met Professor Cornelia de Lange quite unexpectedly. He managed to have a talk with her and tell her of his fears. She was deeply concerned for the young teacher who confided in her, and she visited his home a week later. After examining Jan Maarten thoroughly, she stated that this was a severe case of mongolism and that the child was unlikely ever to be able to walk or talk. She advised his father *not* to keep him at home but to look around for a good institution in which to place him as soon as possible. She also strongly advised him against telling the mother. 'Let her come to realize it herself.'

The father took Professor de Lange home and then tried to live with this knowledge that he alone had. Fortunately he did not succeed, and so the time came when two people were forced to face a catastrophe which they had no choice but to accept and to learn to live with.

Outside their small home the war went on, bringing to each individual his own personal tragedies, sometimes small, sometimes overwhelming.

'Hasn't God given us our grief in a very dear form?' It was this thought which crystallized in the minds of his father and mother after a while. And because they were both very active people, they started discussing what they could actually *do*, what was humanly possible to do to stimulate Jan Maarten's development.

The summer of 1941 found them in a cottage on the banks of a lake. For a Friesian yacht was the third party in the happy triangle of their marriage. It was all the young couple possessed and every holiday was built round this single worldly treasure. The wide, flat meadows of Holland stretched out around the playpen in which Jan Maarten began to develop his first activities. Had the air of a big city disagreed with him? Was the seafaring blood inherited from his father beginning to stir in his veins? The quiet, apathetic baby came alive and started crawling with gusto.

In September his father and mother decided to consult a paediatrician, since it was obvious that they would need expert advice regularly. They chose a specialist who had studied medicine with Jan Maarten's grandfather, and he was relieved at being able to speak his mind quite openly to the young couple. They kept themselves carefully in check, they wanted to know the worst, but they also wanted to know how much they dared to hope. In the two months that had passed since

13

Professor de Lange's visit, Jan Maarten had grown into a lively, cheerful baby. So the prospects the doctor now unfolded were not as sombre as they had been.

'These children are fond of music, they can learn to talk a little, they are very lovable but they are also very delicate. You really shouldn't count on the little boy's reaching his ninth year.' And then came the point which he went into most deeply. 'Do *not* keep the child at home. There are excellent institutions where such children are really happy. It isn't easy to send the child away, but it is better to do so. Better for the mother and better for the other children, when there are other children in the family.'

We all know that bad burns are seldom immediately painful. And this new knowledge was like a bad burn. So the father and mother were able to carry on the conversation with deceptive ease, but it took time to accept these facts and the process of acceptance was a painful one. However, the young couple again proved that the truth sets you free. It is *good* to know the worst. Every thinking person has a right to know it. It is not easy to arrive at conclusions about things it hurts even to talk about. Yet it is not always kindness to spare another's feelings – you could start sparing your own. On the other hand some decisions need time to mature. And when they are put into words they often seem surprisingly simple.

The mother and father came to two conclusions

in a comparatively short time. They formulated them as promises, which they have always kept, and worded them something like this:

'If it is not granted us to keep this child for long, let us consciously each day enjoy every lovely thing he brings us and let us not plan too far ahead.'

This then was an interpretation of 'have no care for the morrow' which Jan Maarten taught them to respect. It helped them to experience each moment intensely and with the utmost perception. It was a decision on which to some extent they based the philosophy of life which supported them in good times and in bad. The second promise concerned the straightforward advice not to keep Jan Maarten at home.

'If ever our home should come to resemble a hospital or if the other children should in any way suffer from their brother's handicap, then Jan Maarten will have to go to an institution. We shall look around for a suitable one, so that if and when the time comes for him to go we shall not have to take decisions in a hurry. But as long as the problems are only organizational ones, we shall not avoid them, but will tackle them boldly.'

The two young people felt strangely at peace, actively at peace if that were possible, and very close to each other. They were safe in the knowledge that underneath them were the Everlasting Arms, and that gave them strength, even in time of war.

The paediatrician glanced quickly round the room.

'That little table in the corner is rather low for a child like this,' was his practical advice. 'And I doubt whether books so near the ground will be safe . . . However, you must see how it works out. Prevention is better than cure.'

Opinions differ as to when the wisdom of a proverb should be put into practice. Jan Maarten had soon learned to crawl in the lakeside cottage. Back in the flat in town a gate was fitted at the top of the stairs, but no other alterations were made. A few days after their arrival, Jan Maarten's mother found him beside the bookcase, picking at the cover of one of the books. She sat down beside him, took his chubby little hand and smacked it gently.

'Don't do that,' she said firmly, and put the book back on the shelf.

Jan Maarten was deposited elsewhere in the room with a toy. His mother went to the kitchen, and when she returned he was again poking in the bookcase but looked up as she came in.

'Don't do that,' she repeated calmly, picked him up and put him in his playpen. This gave him

Seven weeks

Two years

Two years

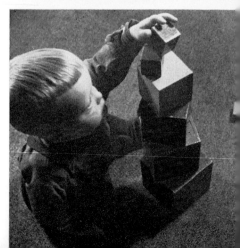

Two years

food for thought, but after a while he turned round and started playing with the toys in the playpen.

Thus the pattern evolved naturally. A light smack on the hand unmistakably linked with the 'sin' committed, was the first step, prompt removal to the playpen the second. The mother found that it was very little trouble to teach him what was allowed and what was not. The golden rule was always to act in the same way even when he only 'tried it on'. He would sometimes sit near the bookcase and look at her. Then he looked at his hand, again at his mother and then slowly reached out for his favourite book. As soon as he touched it, retribution would follow in the form of a rap over the knuckles and a stern 'Don't do that!' (accompanied, of course, by a perfectly straight face). He always seemed relieved that the sequence of events occurred as he had expected.

When the first snowflakes of the severe winter of 1942 started falling in February, the coal shortage in the Province of Utrecht drove three small cousins to the refuge of the warm flat where Jan Maarten and his parents lived. There were twins, just turned two, and a 'big' boy of four.

For the first time Jan Maarten's universal good-will expressed itself in a violent preference for certain individuals. He could not share the play-pen with one of the twins who would not leave him alone, whereas his relations with the other twin were quite normal. During the two months that the cold kept those welcome but involuntary guests, Jan Maarten's forehead was covered with bruises. After all, affection expressed with wooden blocks is apt to leave its mark. Apart from this, all went well.

The mother saw in these weeks that Jan Maarten learned best by imitating. The twins were not yet toilet-trained, so Jan Maarten learned the proper use of the pot, together with them, encouraged by sincere and fervent praise for their united efforts. The snow, the sledge, the many coats and caps did not cause any problems because there were always four little boys who were always doing the same thing. It was a happy time, and Jan Maarten missed his cousins sadly when they left.

What had he learned from them? It was difficult to put it into words. He had shared completely in their games and quarrels; they had knocked him down and put him on his feet again. They had snatched away his toys and given them back again – sometimes. He had learned a number of things *with* them, so his mother realized that it was easier for him that way. But above all Jan Maarten had learned that in a community, however small, every member must be tolerant. Where can you learn that better than in the restricted space of a playpen?

In May 1942 the family returned to the lakeside cottage. Jan Maarten's health again improved

18

careful, don't fall. Come along now. No, Jan Maarten, you mustn't crawl. Naughty boy.'

They never tired of teaching him. Sometimes they went rowing together or sailing, but Jan Maarten remained the big attraction even though he did not seem to make much progress on the uneven grass. However, one day during a thunderstorm came the big surprise. Everyone had rushed inside while the lightning flashed over the lake against a sky as black as ink and the rain still held off. The children sat on the floor with Jan Maarten. They had had to break off their favourite game but now that all the grown-ups were safely settled with a cup of tea, they went on as if nothing had happened.

'Jan Maarten, come along, Jan Maarten. Ooh, aren't you a big boy now.'

The grown-ups looked up, surprised at the warm proud, motherly tones of the nine-year old girl. 'There you are, love. You walk to Eppie now.' Carefully but confidently Jan Maarten moved his feet in the direction of her little brother. He has always found in success and applause enormous stimulus and, after all, he is by no means unique in that. He practised with admirable perseverance, and before long he was able to walk well outside too and go shopping with his mother.

Now that he was walking, a new problem arose at the lakeside cottage: *water*. Up to now water had been a great friend. He loved to go sailing with his parents. He was then put into the harness belonging to his high chair which was fastened to the sheet-block with a fairly long rope. In this way he could climb on to the seat on either side of the boat. Of course he occasionally slid off, but he was astonishingly brave and he learned from his bruises. From his earliest years he seemed to have a sixth sense which warned him in precarious situations and which prompted him to act always in the same way whatever happened: he kept himself in the background, let the grown-ups cope with the situation, did exactly what he was told and did not utter a sound.

'Sit still and don't whine.'

Was it the intonation of the voice? Whatever it was, he understood. When the sail had to be struck suddenly because of a faulty manoeuvre, when mother rushed from one end of the boat to the other and father had his hands full, Jan Maarten sat as quiet as a mouse, almost invisible under the mainsail. And when the sail was hoisted again, the yachtsmen remembered the existence of their exemplary son who was calmly trying to stand up now that the barometer seemed to indicate fair again.

'You're a jolly good sailor,' said his father proudly. Yes, water was a friend. But at the cottage there was no fence between the garden and the water, so a more spacious version of his playpen was put up on the lawn with brown tarpaulin on the ground to keep out the damp. Jan Maarten hated it, and obviously found it just lifted the child onto her hip and carried her around the house wherever she went. She was determined that the little girl should learn to stop crying, that the feeling that she was safe should grow into certainty.

Jan Maarten found the situation rather bewildering at first. He seemed to like the little girl, but of course it was difficult to prevent his feeling neglected. His mother did indeed have two hips, but could hardly get on with her housework carrying two children around with her. Fortunately it soon became evident that Jan Maarten was going to be an important aid on the road to normality for this child who had been deprived in every possible way. Young as she was she quickly realized that what he could do, she could do too. It annoyed her to see him stand up whenever he heard the biscuit tin rattle and move in the direction of that tempting sound. She learned to crawl in record time and was soon standing up on her tiny legs. Jealousy proved a powerful stimulus.

After six weeks the real foster-mother arrived, rather pale but quite ready to take charge of the little girl. It was better not to transfer the child immediately to yet other surroundings, so Jan Maarten and his parents spent another fortnight in the cottage. When they went back to town, the new foster mother and child were to stay on in the cottage. Those few weeks were unforgettable.

Jan Maarten was a good-natured child who liked a joke. For the first time in his life he had some one to play with on his own level. The two children understood each other and had fun together about things that were a mystery to the grown-ups. One evening they sat together on mother's bed playing peek-a-boo with a minute pair of pants belonging to the little girl. Their laughter was heart-warming.

Jan Maarten turned two during this time, and his father was to bring a real birthday cake from town. When mother opened the box a sticky ruin met her eye. Father was indignant. After all, he had held the box upside down only once and then only for a short time – it had no business to collapse like that! After some ingenious plastering the damage was repaired and an impressive cake appeared on the table. Jan Maarten raised both hands above his head in speechless joy. His cake? Really for him? He brought his hands down hard, right in the middle of the cake, from sheer happiness. There must have been a jinx on it!

The departure for town could no longer be postponed, for Jan Maarten's real sister began to announce her arrival. What with one thing and another, it was an eventful autumn for Jan Maarten. The nurse was rather awkward with the little mongoloid child, and mother was of course confined to her bed for the first few days and did not have much time for him. He reacted

26

by wetting his bed. He also became restless at night, as he had been after the little Jewish girl's arrival. Then too there had been an unquiet fortnight, during which he had kicked his blankets aside and knocked his head rhythmically against the side of his crib. His parents were not used to such behaviour; until now he had spoiled them, for even when the house had been so full of guests that his cot had had to be moved into the passage at night, he had not lost a moment's sleep.

As soon as the mother was up and about again, he stopped wetting. She was greatly relieved to discover that this lapse was his way of taking revenge for the neglect he must have felt directly after the birth of his sister. She silently thanked her temporary foster-child for helping her to realize Jan Maarten's great need for her constant, loving attention. He never showed any signs of aggressive jealousy towards his little sister. On the contrary, he considered himself her protector, especially when he was allowed to hold her in his chubby little arms.

That winter Jan Maarten started playing with blocks for hours on end. He would unwearyingly build the most improbable towers. His father and mother, both of whom had studied physics, were astonished at his achievements and positively relieved when the structures eventually collapsed. But he would immediately start all over again, and with great perseverance he taught him-

27

self to build his edifices higher and higher. He also derived evident pleasure from music at this stage. His parents acquired a piano and it was a tremendous success. He marched in time and with a true sense of rhythm to the many tunes that were played, chanting gruffly in his deep little voice. It was the beginning of a firm friendship with music, which for him meant mainly rhythm and movement.

His days were busy that winter, since he could now go shopping with his mother in the neighbourhood. The baker, the butcher, the grocer all lived just round the corner, close enough to home for him to exercise his little legs getting there and back. This meant his first introduction to the world outside the shelter of home. The year before, when he was still in his pram, he had attracted much less notice. There were a lot of children in the neighbourhood, and his mother considered it important that they should understand Jan Maarten. Whenever she passed a group of children playing in the street and they suddenly stopped to stare at the little boy, she would make a point of not hurrying by. She always stopped and let him go up to them, as he invariably wanted to do. She would tell the children his name and ask them theirs.

'Is he ill?' they would ask. 'What is the matter with him?'

The children were naturally interested and asked their questions in a spontaneous, friendly way.

28

'No, he isn't ill,' his mother would then answer. 'But he isn't like you and me. He'll never be a big boy like Leo there. He was born like this. It's a pity, but he is a dear little boy. He has a heart of gold.'

The children would look at him again with interest. His mother remembers that not a single child ever showed a sign of revulsion when confronted with the abnormal boy, as some adults did. Nor did they ever tease him. The children explained to one another what was the matter with him, were always friendly towards him and soon came to accept him completely. Sometimes they worried about him, thinking that his mother did not look after him carefully enough.

Mother came to realize that she would never have got to know so many children if it had not been for Jan Maarten, nor would she have seen the best side of their nature as she did. Once a little girl of five was waiting for her at the lamp-post at the corner, pretending to play hopscotch.

'Can't he ever get better?' she asked earnestly, as one grown-up to another.

'No,' said his mother, 'no, that's not possible.'

'But I think that's awful,' she cried out indignantly, with tears in her eyes.

'So do I,' said his mother. 'But you must remember one thing. You and I can be unhappy about it, but look at him. He's very happy, he really is never sad. He laughs and enjoys life.

Then we mustn't be sad either, must we?'
The little girl hopped a few steps, pondering
deeply. She sighed and said 'No, not really, eh
Jan Maarten?' and she bent over him with a
gentle, motherly, protective gesture that was
moving to see. You can learn much from a five-
year-old.

Father and mother both came from big families,
so Jan Maarten has many cousins, some older,
some younger, all of whom liked coming to stay.
They play with, but specially around, Jan Maarten.
When they were of the age of the little girl at the
lamp-post mother would explain to them about
the boy. They inevitably appreciated this and
often wanted to ask questions about certain
things that bothered them. These talks invariably
contributed to the success of their visit. It was as
if the 'Jan Maarten question' could now be put
among the problems settled satisfactorily in their
minds.
He met not only the children in the neighbourhood, but the adults too. Sometimes when a
group of women stood discussing the latest news
at the street corner, Jan Maarten would suddenly
squeeze his way into the middle of the circle with
an expression on his face which clearly said 'If
there's anything interesting going on here, I'd
like to know what it is!' His mother found these
situations painful, but the child was so quick, and
often wriggled out of her grasp before she

realized what he was doing. But the sequel to his behaviour was invariably the same: the strained worried faces relaxed as they looked down at the little mongoloid child. Even their voices sounded friendlier.

'Hallo, sonny,' 'Oh, poor lamb.' 'Well, what have you got to say, my lad?'

His mother nodded gratefully to them as she picked up the stray 'lamb'. Very occasionally the subject would be mentioned, usually at the end of a long conversation. The greengrocer's wife would say:

'It's a crying shame, it is.'

'Oh, he's a dear little boy, and there are more terrible things in the world today.'

'My dear, a truer word was never said.'

Yes, the time we lived in then reduced our problem to its proper proportions.

Each year mother moved to the cottage in the country earlier in the year. She was fond of the flat in town, but the fresh air was good for the children, and the almost inaccessible spot by the lakeside was a safe retreat in war-time for the father and many of their friends and relations.

In the spring of 1943 Jan Maarten's sister showed signs of becoming a precocious young thing, which gave the mother moments of anxiety. But her fears were unfounded; Jan Maarten taught his sister manners in the most Christian way possible. As soon as she could crawl, and that was very soon, she upset all his games. If he sat playing quietly with a car, she would snatch it from him. He would watch her for a moment, turn round, take another toy from the cupboard and start playing with that without taking any notice of her. But she had other ideas. She would wriggle up to him and wrench the new toy from his hands. Philosophically Jan Maarten would take up the original motor car and push it gently over the mat. This was the ideal way of curing his sister of her whims. In a very short time they were playing together harmoniously and have done so ever since.

Father and mother read everything they could lay hands on about mongolism and they arrived at the following conclusions. Since according to the literature on the subject, the I.Q. of a mongol is somewhere between 40 and 45 and Jan Maarten's could therefore be assumed to be in the neighbourhood of 50, it was reasonable to expect him to behave like a child of half his age. And that meant that for the time being they could set the same standard for him and for his younger sister, especially as regards what they were and were not allowed to do. On that point Jan Maarten was even a help for he accepted discipline and had a fitting sense of right and wrong.

It is a great mistake to misuse the prolonged babyhood of mongoloid children by spoiling them, since the effects of spoiling can seldom be eradicated. It is definitely *easy* to teach these

Eighteen months

Three years

Five years

Photo: Cas Oorthuys

Ten years

children rules of good behaviour because they thrive on praise. From an early age Jan Maarten always tidied up, first his playpen and later the toy cupboard. Of course his mother was glad that she did not have to do it, and he was so happy and proud at being praised that the habit was formed for life.

That summer he began to talk. His first word was 'Heit' (the Friesian for father) which he practised day-in day-out in the orchard, making his father as proud as a peacock. The other children were to follow his example, and later 'Heit' and 'Mem' became family usage. Jan Maarten added 'Mem' to his monosyllabic repertoire a whole month after he had learned to say 'Heit'.

His sister did not lag far behind, but when, at the age of eight months, she unexpectedly caught scarlet fever (there was an epidemic at the time), Jan Maarten was able to forge ahead again. Shortly afterwards, however, he had a setback which almost cost him his life. His mother was also down with scarlet fever and his father recovered from a severe attack of quinsy just in time to discover a red mark on his son's body that made him suspect erysipelas. The village doctor, who was doing a superhuman job visiting his many scattered patients on a bicycle, confirmed the suspicion, and together they saved the sick child. A friend with nursing experience came to look after the mother and daughter. At last, when everyone had recovered, the family returned to town profoundly grateful that they had survived this ordeal.

During the winter the problem of Jan Maarten's restless nights became more acute. He would roll to the edge of his crib in his sleep and thump his head rhythmically against the wooden side for hours on end. At the same time he would kick aside his blankets and so caught cold time and again. His mother and father were both sound sleepers. They did not mind getting out of bed several times a night to cover up their little son, but in the long run it exhausted them. The paediatrician considered this a clear indication that the time had come to find a suitable home for Jan Maarten. Apart from prescribing sleeping pills, which made no difference at all, he was unable to help the parents. They were both tired from lack of sleep and did not want to take so momentous a decision until they felt physically capable of doing so. And so a nurse was engaged for the first time in Jan Maarten's life to sit with him at night for a few weeks. She had trained in psychiatric hospitals, and so in her eyes there was very little the matter with Jan Maarten. They took to each other immediately and she treated him as if he were a normal child. The parents were as relieved at this as they were at being able to have nights of unbroken rest again. When the nurse left after those few weeks, Jan Maarten missed her sorely. He sat despondently on her bed saying 'Och, dillekie, och dillekie.' This, his version of the word 'sister', became her nickname when she returned to the family in the autumn; they had asked her to spend a fortnight with them towards the end of the summer holidays of 1944, for Jan Maarten had longed to see her again. A severe railway strike broke out during her stay and kept her a prisoner at the lakeside cottage. And again it was her relaxed and friendly interest in all that Jan Maarten did that made her an ideal companion in the darkest winter of the war.

An inspired idea about Jan Maarten's sleeping arrangements brought relief to the whole family that summer. He was still thumping his head against the side of his crib, disturbing the whole household. Now the frame on which the mattress rested was tied to four ropes which were hung on four hooks in the ceiling. A fisherman friend made a net big enough to form four 'walls' around the mattress. Jan Maarten now swung a few inches from the floor in a modified version of a hammock and loved it. The first three nights he crept up to the bedhead in his sleep, but as there was nothing to hit his head against, he merely tumbled half an inch off the mattress and sat in the net, his head still on his pillow, fast asleep. After that he no longer crawled out from under the blankets. He tried thumping his head in the pillow, which disturbed nobody, but that did not seem to afford him much satisfaction, and the habit gradually died a natural death. Jan Maarten slept in this hammock for nearly fifteen months. The parents screwed hooks into the ceiling of every room in the house so that the hammock could be moved as required. This was a great advantage at a time when the cottage had to be as elastic as possible, since men and women hiding from the Occupation Authorities were coming and going almost daily.

By the autumn of 1944 number three was well on the way. The baby, a boy, was born at the beginning of the blackest winter the country had known. He was welcomed by the whole family and Jan Maarten was a real big brother as he sat on a low stool holding the newcomer in his arms. As the winter drew on the baby had increasing difficulty in breathing. It was not easy to explain to the doctor what was worrying the father and mother and it was only when the fits occurred several times an hour that the doctor was able to diagnose something definite. There was no cure, and six months after his birth, Jan Maarten's brother passed away peacefully. When mother had laid the baby in his crib for the last time, she walked back slowly to the other children. Jan Maarten came to meet her and his grief seemed almost adult. As his mother knelt down in front of him, he took her head in his hands, gazed into her face and laid her head gently on his shoulder:

36

'Och memmekie, och memmekie,' his deep little voice consoled.

From now on Jan Maarten's mother and father were convinced that his intelligence quotient of barely 50 was more than compensated by a 'quotient' of the heart far above average.

III

The end of the war in May 1945 left much sorrow in our little village. Many people had died, whose passing we still commemorate annually and for whom we still mourn. The German army retreated past the peaceful cottage for days and nights on end, while the children ran repeatedly to the bridge to watch all these men passing by.

A small cousin was, for a while, the youngest child in the house. She had been roaming with her parents from place to place, for they had been unable to stay in their home after the railway strike. She joined the family at the cottage in the spring. The house was rather full as usual, and Jan Maarten was good and happy with so much going on around him. His speech improved, but at a much slower rate than that of his sister.

What were the parents to do when he got angry or was disobedient? They fully agreed with each other that he should *not* be slapped. He was exceptionally strong and should on no account be punished in a manner he might be tempted to try out on his little sister. Words of praise and words of warning influenced his behaviour most effectively, but what words of warning were to be used now that the slap was to be a thing of the past? The next corrective measure to be introduced was the cold-water tap. At five Jan Maarten was still small and light enough to be carried swiftly to the nearest tap and have his head held under it if the situation so required. The treatment astonished him but also seemed to release some tension in him. A few drops of water on his flaxen hair were soon enough to convince him that he was heading in the wrong direction.

Jan Maarten's father and mother were now faced with decisions that were to affect the rest of their lives. His father started a new job and they decided to live permanently in the country. A cottage in the country and a flat in town was a luxury they could no longer permit themselves, with so many houses destroyed in the war. At first the mother was upset by the thought of living permanently in the mildewed, primitive surroundings which she had readily accepted in the last few years of the war. Two considerations, however, made her change her mind. The father had basically always been a country man who discovered in the war how much he relaxed and enjoyed every free moment he could spend in the open air. And then every real step forward Jan Maarten had made seemed to be due to living in the country. Later on his mother came to love the countryside for itself.

Now that they had come to live permanently in the village, they were soon allocated a better and more solidly built house. There, in the midst of paint-pots and ladders, 'Heit' and 'Mem' celebrated their 'pewter' wedding anniversary (a Dutch tradition), remembering the six-and-a-quarter years of unforgettable experiences and rejoicing that they had arrived safely so far, in the harbour of peace.

Jan Maarten and his sister 'sailed' through the empty house on a wooden tray. Heit and Mem toasted each other in tea and the festive biscuits lay on pewter plates. There was a beautiful view over the lakes from the big window in the living-room.

But what was Jan Maarten thinking of? He stood in the middle of the room, holding a wooden block in his hand in the inimitable way all boys have and all girls would like to be able to.

'Jan Maarten, don't throw that block.'

The tone of mother's voice left no room for doubt.

He looked at her triumphantly and threw with all his might. The block landed right in the middle of the irreplacable window-pane that trembled in its frame from the force of the blow, but miraculously survived the onslaught. Everyone was relieved, but what next? Mother marched up to Jan Maarten and took him firmly by the hand. He let himself be led off, realizing as he did that crime and punishment were inevitably linked. His mother thought hard and quickly as she propelled him out of the house; she had to think quickly of a suitable punishment for deliberate naughtiness that could be established as a precedent in the new house. As they reached the garage, her eye fell on the tap. As if this had been the sole object of the expedition, she held the boy with clothes and all under the jet of cold water. He did not utter a sound, but when she released him, he burst into tears and flung himself into her arms. They sat together, equally shocked, for a moment before mother fetched dry clothes for him. During the coming year, whenever he contemplated any naughtiness, one movement in the direction of the garage was usually enough to make him change his mind.

Shortly after the family moved, Jan Maarten's youngest sister was born. In the beginning neither he nor his elder sister saw anything of the baby, since they were both suffering from a mild attack of whooping cough, which was fortunately immediately recognized as such by the doctor. The baby was kept quite separate from the other two.

That summer there were a number of things that kept him busy. Since the garden of the new house was bigger than that of the cottage, new toys were possible, such as a pedal car and a wooden scooter. Both were a source of endless pleasure. And then there was the wooden rocking-horse, which seemed to fulfil some need in the child. It was as if the pent-up energy that he had formerly expended in thumping his head against the side of his bed could now be released through his entire body in rhythmic rocking and singing. After a while either Mem or the nurse would distract his attention with something else for fear of his going on too long, but a certain amount of rhythmic movement every day obviously did him good.

There was a lot of illness that summer; jaundice, inflammation of the middle ear, and quinsy attacked the whole family. Heit and Mem did not therefore immediately notice that Jan Maarten was growing moodier and moodier. His natural good temper and his chivalrous behaviour towards his younger sisters and cousins were beginning to deteriorate. Soon, his parents realized that he was getting grumpy and obstinate, and they decided to keep an eye on him. Perhaps the time had come to seek admittance to a home?

This was the first time that the question had arisen seriously and the parents faced it squarely. They decided to consult their doctor on the advisability of taking him to a paediatrician or a child psychiatrist. It was essential that the other children should not suffer from any new development that might be taking place in Jan Maarten. The doctor had become a good friend of the family and he gave Jan Maarten a check-up before committing himself. He found that the sturdy, apple-cheeked child was suffering from acute anaemia: the haemoglobin content of his blood was down to forty-five.

'Oh madam,' said the maid, 'no wonder the poor child is always crotchety.'

She was speaking from experience, for she too was anaemic and was sometimes so tired she could hardly drag herself through the house.

It was not easy to help Jan Maarten over this obstacle, and anaemia remained one of the weak spots in the frail armour of his health. Fortunately his temper improved rapidly and he was soon his old sunny self again. For the first time his parents noticed a definite trait that manifested itself later time and again: whenever Jan Maarten was unhappy or moody, there was always something physically wrong and usually radically wrong at that. He did not give in readily and he wanted to be well and strong. He therefore never gave warning by being listless, but just suddenly caved in, at which point it was high time to do something about him.

It was fortunate that the anaemia belonged to the past by the time Jan Maarten was old enough to go to school. Although education was not compulsory for backward children in 1947, father and mother agreed that they should not delay in sending him, even though he was still very babyish in his ways. They first approached the Sisters of St. Ursula at Nieuwveen to inquire if they would consider taking a little Protestant mongoloid

43

child as a day-boy. This was a novelty for the Sisters and they were not enthusiastic. During the parents' first visit, Sister Paula showed them through the school which she helped to found and from which she was about to retire. She was obviously a woman of great practical wisdom and warmth, and her advice to the disappointed parents was that they should come back in a month's time with Jan Maarten.

'It is an unusual and therefore difficult case for Mother Superior,' she explained. 'She must be allowed plenty of time to make up her mind.'

A month later father, mother and Jan Maarten presented themselves at the convent a second time. They were not very hopeful, but the intensely loving and happy atmosphere of the convent had made such a deep impression on them that they felt they had to try again, even if their journey was to be in vain. They sat anxiously in the waiting-room where the sunlight was tempered by the tall, ancient trees in the sheltered garden outside. The door opened to admit Sister Eugenia, the school's secretary. Jan Maarten ran up to her on his chubby little legs and grasped the full black skirts of her habit. He was intrigued by this new phenomenon in his life.

'Mem,' he asked, 'what kind of a man is this?'

Heit and Mem felt like children who'd committed some dreadful *faux pas*, but Sister Eugenia's eyes were smiling. She mentioned the long waiting-list for the boarding-school and spoke about the

44

many children then attending the school who did not really belong there.

'We are really a teaching order,' she explained, 'not a nursing order. During the war we accepted many children whom we knew were incapable of being taught anything. But we had to hide them from the Germans, who fortunately never came here. And of course we can't now suddenly turn away those little ones who are patients.'

Father pleaded at this point that Jan Maarten would be present in class only, that he would be brought to school every day and fetched again and that he would not be taking another child's place in the boarding establishment. His arguments carried noticeably more weight than on the previous occasion. Sister Eugenia retired to consult Mother Superior. She stayed away a long time and came back shaking her head. The parents prepared themselves for a disappointment; who better than they were aware of the difficulties?

'Mother Superior is not sure whether to accept your proposal definitely,' said Sister Eugenia. 'She feels we should try it out until Christmas and then we can both see if the arrangement works.'

And so began a period of nine years in Jan Maarten's life which was of inestimable value for him and for the whole family.

IV

It is impossible to tell the story of Jan Maarten's schooldays without first uttering heartfelt thanks to the Sisters whom we came to know at St. Ursula's, Nieuwveen. What a remarkable group of dedicated women! There was not one of whom we could not say 'This is the right woman in the right place.' And the joy with which they carried out each task! When Mem made some remark about the class of mongoloid children to Jan Maarten's first teacher, she looked at her openly and cheerfully.

'Do you know, Mrs. de Vries, it is a privilege for us to work among these children. They are God's fairest flowers.'

And the Sisters accept this privilege naturally and gladly and effortlessly.

The first time Jan Maarten's sister went with her mother to fetch him from school, Sister Miriam knelt down in front of her and said from the fullness of her heart, 'You almost forget here that they can look like this. Mrs. de Vries, how beautiful children are, like angels.'

But she stood up again almost immediately and returned cheerfully to her 'fairest flowers'.

During the time Jan Maarten spent there, St.

Ursula's had several different Mothers Superior, but Sister Eugenia saw him all the way through. He had four excellent teachers and there was always a fifth Sister in the background who supervised the meals and breaks with true motherly devotion.

The value of these harmonious surroundings to Jan Maarten and the other mongoloid children at Nieuwveen was incalculable. And the parents of these children are wholly convinced that the Sisters of St. Ursula will in due time be rewarded by their Maker.

Jan Maarten started school in September, 1947. Four days a week he was on the road along the River Amstel to Nieuwveen before eight in the morning, early enough to enable his sister to be taken to infant school afterwards. He was home by a quarter to five in the afternoon. He stayed at home on Wednesdays, for his mother was afraid that the long days might prove too much for him. There was no school on Saturdays.

In the beginning the new venture seemed to be an unqualified success, but difficulties arose before long. He went through stages of kicking, pricking people with pins and screaming, which could always be traced to a new arrival in the class who had behaved in this way.

'Oh, Mrs. de Vries, when that happens you have them all kicking within a week,' said Sister Miriam.

For weeks on end Jan Maarten pretended he could not walk and lurched from the wall to the nearest chair in a masterly fashion. The urge to imitate and the virtuosity with which he expressed this urge were the source of both his progress and his misbehaviour. He came to accept discipline more readily, but he also began to grow aware of his own wishes.

This was the beginning of a remarkable period. He would be playing and the time would come for him to tidy up. But Jan Maarten did not want to stop his game.

'All right, Jan Maarten, I'll wait.'

The grown-up concerned then stood obviously waiting. He could not bear the tension that this created and gave in sooner or later; in fact, he found it terrible. He often said, 'No, don't wait, I'll come now,' which he did indeed do. This waiting became the next disciplinary measure and one that was a strain to both mother and child. It was another aid in the process of learning to obey, but one that could not be used indiscriminately. With every new discovery in the sphere of discipline there was always the danger of it being used too frequently, or for unimportant reasons, not so much by the parents as by the other members of the household who wanted to see if it really worked. The mother made a habit of discussing such matters with the younger children, sometimes forbidding them to interfere. Something that meant punishment for Jan Maarten

Ten years

Ten years

could not be allowed to deteriorate into a game. At the end of his first school year the parents discussed with the Sisters the difficulties that were arising at home through Jan Maarten's imitating new pupils. After much thought it was decided to move him to a class that was really rather above his standard, but at least he stopped acquiring bad habits. Now the Sisters had always said that when a child was placed in a new class it took him about a year to get used to a new teacher, and only when he had done so, would he start making progress again. But Jan Maarten did not advance even after the first year; the class really was too difficult for him.

There were other important events in his life during this period. He had always liked parties and outings and particularly enjoyed a visit to the fair. There he discovered his ideal in the shape of a small bicycle on a roundabout on which he was allowed to ride for a long time for about a penny. This experience inspired him with a great longing for a real bicycle. He did not often want something badly, but when he did, there was no getting him to change his mind.

His father's first comparatively long trip abroad took place in 1947. On the day of his return, as soon as he had been welcomed, Jan Maarten took his hand and asked, 'May I go for a drive with you?' Heit was surprised at his asking but pleased that Jan should show this initiative, and he promised to take him for a ride round the block before dinner. Jan Maarten appeared to have a definite purpose in mind. He wanted to go to a certain garage near the house of some friends of the family, a garage his father occasionally used. In the window was a green model jeep. When they arrived home with this, Mem was speechless.

'Did he ask for it?' she inquired incredulously, for Jan Maarten never asked for anything for himself.

'No,' replied Heit. 'He just told me I had to pay for it!'

Two years passed by and Jan Maarten had become obsessed by the idea of the bicycle he had ridden at the fair. His obsession was like a latent disease that keeps recurring. The family spent the month of June at the seaside. At the beginning of the village there was a bicycle shop, and mother had to make a detour whenever they went to the beach, for Jan Maarten could not be enticed away from the shop window in which 'his' bicycle was displayed. When asked what he wanted for his birthday, he could list only three things: a bicycle, crayons, and peppermints. Father and mother gave way and decided to buy a strong children's bicycle.

'After all, the girls can use it later,' they said. 'He'll be proud just to walk next to it holding the handlebars as he did with the scooter at first.'

50

Little could they guess what would happen.

On 22 October he wheeled his new bicycle outside in a state of trance, mounted it and rode off down the garden path. The only thing he found difficult was dismounting, so the parents placed up-turned crates all over the garden, and that solved the problem. It was the first toy he did not willingly share with his sister. He allowed her to have a ride, but always stood waiting to take possession of his property again. For the first time something really belonged to him. No one grudged him the sole ownership of this long-coveted new toy, but he was encouraged to be 'noble' about letting others have a turn at riding it.

There was a steady stream of visitors to the house by the lake-side and Jan Maarten soon learned to be a good host.

'Shall I take your coat? Would you like a cup of tea? Do sit down, I'll go and call Mem.'

His naturally friendly disposition prompted this politeness, and he liked to make his contribution to the pleasant atmosphere in the home. Perhaps that was the motive for his obedience, which always had a beneficial effect on the younger guests. On the other hand he learned a great deal from being treated like one of the others. When his father showed a film he had made on one of his trips abroad and the adults occupied all the available chairs, a single clear command:

'Children onto the floor – get a move on, Jan

Maarten, you too!' was enough to make him take his place among the other youngsters.

The simplest solution to a problem is usually the most obvious one, and we discovered this when the problem of Jan Maarten's restlessness at night arose. He had always slept very restlessly; he would kick aside the covers in his sleep and consequently caught cold. He then had to be nursed back to health and the process started all over again. This had worried his nurse for some time, and when the family moved to the new house directly after the war, she asked for a large double bed for herself and Jan Maarten; she would then immediately be able to take action if he lay uncovered. That was a tremendous improvement, but Mem could not help feeling that it was the wrong solution and one that could not be permanent. After long deliberation, the simple idea of making a sleeping bag was born. It consisted of a very roomy bag made of two blankets pleated at the top and sewn to a strip of strong linen onto which an inner bag of sheeting could be sewed. The top of the bag could also be loosely drawn together by means of four pairs of strings. The sleeping bag was tried out during a seaside holiday and served its purpose admirably. Once it came into use, Jan Maarten no longer caught cold at night.

In the spring of 1950 Mem discussed a new plan with the Sisters at St. Ursula's. Once a month

Jan Maarten's nurse was allowed to spend a day at school. She helped the Sister in the class and followed her methods closely. The same books and teaching aids were bought, and from then on Jan Maarten was able to work at home with his nurse with the same material and in the same way as at school. Every day he was away from school he spent an hour doing lessons and so at last began to make gradual progress. *He learned to read and write and to count up to ten.* The Sisters attached great importance to the children's being able to count, since this was a great help later when they started handicraft lessons.

'If they can't tell the difference between two and three threads, there is so little they can be taught.' The following year he had no trouble at all in learning to tell the time. He was always surprising his parents and teachers in this way, as indeed many children at St. Ursula's did.

His visit to the fair had another positive consequence for Jan Maarten: he found a friend there. This boy was six months older than Jan Maarten and the second youngest child in a family living on a farm nearby. His father and mother had been very unfortunate in the beginning. There was nobody to explain why their little boy was different from other children, and they tried all sorts of remedies before some one had the courage to point out that this was not an illness that could be cured. It is particularly difficult to

53

accept this truth about one of your children when the way to its revelation has been paved with broken hopes. The boy was nine when he started going to school with Jan Maarten. He was a healthy child and much more robust than Jan Maarten. He learned to do raffia work perfectly, but he never learned to read and write for he started school three years after Jan Maarten did. He is now happily employed on his father's farm. Is illiteracy such a great handicap for mongoloid children then? Yes, it certainly is. They derive such tremendous enjoyment from reading the newspaper for themselves; Jan Maarten's favourite topics are still the Royal Family and the weather forecast. It gives them great pleasure to be able to write to friends and relations. The course leading to these great sources of pleasure must be embarked upon in good time, and in good time means when the child is about five or six years old. One of the Sisters at St. Ursula's explained why a delay is fatal.

'Our children need the whole of the first year and sometimes the second too to learn to work in a class and to listen to their teacher. *Every year that they are allowed to do as they like at home is doubly lost because it is very difficult to wean them from bad habits.*'

Jan Maarten and his friend now went to school together, usually singing. Jan Maarten knew a great many songs, but his friend's repertoire was much smaller. They did not need to express their affections for each other in words.

There was almost always something not quite in order with Jan Maarten's health. At this stage it was the 'snake's tongue' with which he had been born and which had grown as he grew. It had always been too big for his mouth and there was a lump on the tip which was gradually getting bigger. Jan Maarten was paying regular visits to an orthodontist in Utrecht at this time, and it was he who advised the parents to consult a surgeon about the abnormally long tongue. He did not mince his words.

'If he were my child I would operate on him tomorrow. Of course it is painful, but a tongue heals quickly and it's all over in a fortnight.'

Jan Maarten and his mother went to Hospital together for the first time. Mother was allowed to sleep with him and to do most of the nursing herself after receiving instructions on what to do. She installed a little bit of home in the hospital room.

The operation was painful and the first few days were difficult. But Jan Maarten's faith in mankind in general and in doctors in particular was unshaken. One of the stitches worked loose and it was evident that something would have to be done about it. With a heavy heart mother took her small son to the surgeon again. As soon as he entered the room Jan Maarten got up, took his hand and explained what had happened.

'My tongue isn't quite right. You may do it over

again. I'll sit quite still and they needn't hold me down.'

They came back together after a while, Jan Maarten striding along like a man.

'I hope that will do the trick,' said the doctor. 'But remember, Jan Maarten, no hard things like peppermints and so on, or it'll open up again. Stick to porridge for the time being.'

Jan Maarten nodded earnestly.

'And ice-cream?' he asked.

The doctor burst out laughing.

'Tell your mother you deserve a nice big one.'

Jan Maarten followed the doctor's instructions in an exemplary manner and the tongue healed beautifully.

This made all the difference to him. At home he was taught some deep-breathing exercises and at school he received speech lessons, thanks to the enterprising spirit of Sister Amelberga. A speech therapist had just been appointed at St. Ursula's to help the mongoloid children who had not yet learned to talk. The history of his appointment was interesting. It was believed at that time that a mongoloid child who had not begun to talk before his tenth year would never learn. A young speech therapist decided to test this out. He took a child already above this age limit and taught him to speak within a year. It was typical of St. Ursula's that he was subsequently asked to join their staff. Sister Amelberga promptly proposed that Jan Maarten also be given speech lessons.

'I think it would do him a lot of good,' she said. 'He talks so explosively and he himself must find that unsatisfactory. And now that his tongue no longer hampers him . . .'

No, that obstacle had been removed, and Jan Maarten's speech soon improved.

He was full of jokes which he loved airing. On one occasion he was in the lavatory when he heard noises indicating that somebody was going out. Surely they wouldn't leave without him! The lavatory door was flung open and out shot Jan Maarten. He gave himself a smack on the bottom and cried,

'You stay where you are, I'll send you back by post.'

He got on excellently with his grandfather, who was fond of teasing his grandchildren. Jan Maarten's intelligent little sister was sometimes the victim of Grandpa's practical jokes, for she simply did not expect her bun to disappear from her plate whilst she was helpfully looking round the room for the little bird Grandpa said was there. The whole situation puzzled her but not Jan Maarten. 'And what about the other bird then, Grandpa?' he asked.

'What other bird?' asked Grandpa, surprised.

'The one in your hand with the bun,' he laughed infectiously.

'You bad boy,' sighed Grandpa, but the little girl glanced gratefully at her big brother.

Grandfather would frown when he saw Jan Maarten cross himself after saying grace; his orthodox Calvinist heart found it difficult to accept the Catholic education his grandson was receiving. But when Jan Maarten recited the Lord's Prayer calmly and faultlessly, he was deeply moved, and expressed his appreciation in words that breathed a truly tolerant spirit.

Mother Superior also had her problems concerning her little Protestant pupil.

'May he attend scripture lessons, or would you rather he left the class?' she asked Jan Maarten's parents during one of their visits to St. Ursula's.

'Do you think he'll learn anything wrong?' replied his father.

Mother Superior understood the joke.

'We'll do our best not to let that happen,' she smiled.

A good while later Mother Superior wished to demonstrate to Jan Maarten's parents that he was deriving real benefit from the lessons. Jan Maarten stood before her and she asked him in a friendly manner:

'Tell me, Jan Maarten, what has God given you?'

Jan Maarten racked his brains.

'A soul,' he answered solemnly.

An excellent answer, but Mother Superior was not yet satisfied

'And what else?'

Jan Maarten thought again.

'Chocolate,' he replied in tones of gratitude.

In the summer of 1952 Jan Maarten obtained the swimming certificate of the Royal Netherlands Swimming Association. This was, of course, entirely due to the efforts of a tireless teacher who had coached him regularly during the summer of 1951. In 1952 one of her brothers assisted her and together they made a proficient swimmer out of Jan Maarten.

His first contact with the deep end of the swimming pool was unforgettable. His teacher's brother thought it high time that Jan Maarten started taking swimming seriously, for he always played around in the shallow end and could not be persuaded really to try. He always wore a bathing costume with shoulder straps so that he could be 'fished' out of the water if he got into difficulties; in fact, the swimming pool management insisted on this type of costume being worn by all non-swimmers. The brother decided to try out an experiment with Jan Maarten. With the fishing rod in his hand in case of accidents, he called Jan Maarten to him and gave him a sudden push when the boy was least expecting it. Jan Maarten surfaced and swam to the side in a rage. He climbed out while the brother waited, smiling and pleased at the success of his manoeuvre.

'May I have your rod?' asked Jan Maarten.

The brother handed it over without suspecting

anything, and Jan Maarten bent down to lay it carefully on the ground. From his squatting position he suddenly tackled the unsuspecting young man who landed with clothes and all in the water. Jan Maarten was radiant!

From that time on he was made to practise seriously. By praising him lavishly his clever teachers managed to keep him at it and to improve his performance gradually. And then, one very windy day, he took the test and passed. It was a triumph for all concerned. Jan Maarten was inordinately proud of his certificate and his parents were profoundly relieved that he could now venture near water without risk.

The following spring Jan Maarten and his sisters had their tonsils removed. Mother accompanied the children to the hospital and slept in Jan Maarten's room so that she could look after him as she had done when his tongue was operated upon. His sisters were put in the children's ward. The specialist who performed the operation said that Jan Maarten had been the easiest of the three to handle because he had co-operated with such complete trust. This was a memorable but unpleasant Whitsun for Heit and Mem, but all three children enjoyed themselves. Once his tonsils were removed Jan Maarten was at last rid of his chronic cold.

In the years that followed, the parents realized time and again how delicate Jan Maarten was.

60

When they looked back at this stage in his life, it seemed as if the tonsils had been removed at the last possible moment. They could not have risked the operation at a later stage. *Their inevitable conclusion was that one should never postpone for a handicapped child what is essential for a normal one.*

This year mother spent a month at the seaside with the children. In an ideal cottage the same routine, which was enjoyed by everyone, was resumed every year; every morning they worked and played on the beach, every afternoon a nap was followed by a walk in the woods. Jan Maarten thoroughly enjoyed himself. He played ball and cycled with his sisters. He built sandcastles and paddled. His imagination was extraordinarily fertile. Every morning he came downstairs pretending to be a different person, sometimes a cousin, sometimes the waiter at the hotel where the family occasionally dined during the weekends when father was with them. He was very observant and could imitate surprisingly small details. Very often one glance was enough to reveal who he was pretending to be. Granny accompanied the family every year and got on famously with Jan Maarten when he was in these moods. They all had great fun together.

Mother was worried about the boy during this month and her anxiety increased as time went on. He seemed to have developed the habit of jerking his head compulsively. Was she imagining things?

Father noticed the queer twitch during his week-end visit, too, but they decided to postpone taking action since their doctor was away and the paediatrician was attending a conference abroad. The following week Mem by chance witnessed a little scene that was quite unlike Jan Maarten. He lost his balance while cycling, fell and then jumped up and kicked his bicycle with rage. His pink cheeks and the healthy colour of the inside of his eyelids gave no indication of what was troubling him. A visit to the doctor confirmed that he was again suffering from anaemia. Could that nervous jerk of the head be put down to the same cause? As soon as their good friend the paediatrician returned from Geneva they decided to consult him. He gave the problem careful consideration, and Heit and Mem were to remember this talk time and again in the coming years. The doctor discussed quite frankly the difficult stage Jan Maarten was now approaching. He was a frail craft to keep afloat, and in the coming years the sea of life would be rough and stormy for him. The physical changes about to take place were not likely to be typical of a normal adolescence, though that *could* happen. But his resistance to illness would be greatly lowered and every minor ailment could have grave consequences.

'A doctor can't keep an eye on him for you; after all, you yourselves are specialists in Jan Maarten,' warned their friend. 'Don't hesitate to call in medical advice immediately if anything threatens to go wrong; you owe it to him.'

A neurologist treated Jan Maarten for the twitch and the anaemia was cured. He started growing now too and losing his puppy fat.

That autumn there was an epidemic of a mild type of jaundice, and Jan Maarten was one of the 'victims' – fortunately, for the strict diet, without fat and rich in protein, completely cured the chronic stomach-ache of which he had complained ever since he could talk. He was inordinately pleased and relieved at this, which made him a much easier patient than his sisters, who had to be coaxed gently over their jaundice depression.

This was the period in which Jan Maarten no longer needed a nurse. Once the anaemia was a thing of the past, he slept much more peacefully, and the success of the sleeping bag meant that he did not have to be watched so carefully at night. In 1950 he moved into a bedroom next to that of his parents, who could now keep an eye on him at night without losing too much sleep themselves.

Mem now accompanied Jan Maarten to St. Ursula's once a month. She learned a great deal there and her memories of those days will remain with her all her life. The geography lesson was one such memorable occasion. Jan Maarten was undoubtedly the best pupil in this class, since all those strange names meant something to him.

63

The children were learning the five continents.
'Who knows the name of one of the continents?'
'Europe', answered the class in unison.
'Good. And another one?'
Jan Maarten raised his hand.
'America. Heit has been there.'
'Good. Try again.'
'Australia. Heit and Mem have been there.'
And he proudly showed the class his koala bear.
Africa, Asia, Jan Maarten had heard of them all,
had received letters and picture postcards from
all over the world. Then Europe was dealt with
and the class had their say again.
'Spain, that's where Sinterklaas* lives; Italy is
where the Pope lives.'
Jan Maarten was able to make his contribution
here too happily and proudly, though he was
sometimes too bold.
'The Netherlands is divided into eleven pieces.
You all know that, don't you? Now what do we
call those pieces?'
The class was silent. What *do* we call those pieces?
Jan Maarten raised his hand.
'Proverbs,' he ventured.
Later he and his mother practised the word
'province' over and over again; it was a much
more abstract conception than the Spain of
Sinterklaas.
Among the children at St. Ursula's were also a

*Sinterklaas or St. Nicholas, is to Duch children what
Santa Claus is to English, his traditional home being Spain.

Twelve years

Fourteen years

number from broken homes. As Sinterklaas festivities approached (they are held on 5 December), mother discussed these children with one of the Sisters with a view to providing any little extras that might be needed.

'Are there also mongoloid children in your wards?' asked mother.

'No,' was the reply. 'Mongoloid children don't live to be six under such circumstances.'

This reminded Jan Maarten's mother again how delicate mongoloid children are even when they are born with a sound heart. Many of them have heart defects. Either way, they need loving care at every stage of their lives.

In the spring of 1954 a very special event took place. Jan Maarten, his sisters, Heit and Mem all went on a holiday to Juan les-Pins on the French Riviera. It was a wonderful experience. They almost filled the little *pension*. Jan Maarten's behaviour was exemplary; he was always polite, always thrilled with everything. His talent for mimicry enabled him to imitate French words and phrases faultlessly, and he enjoyed running errands and saying a pleasant word to the waiter or to the elderly guests. When either of his sisters looked at her plate in disgust, Heit and Mem were able to keep in the background.

'Mmm, jolly good,' Jan Maarten would say. 'Merci, monsieur,' – that was to the waiter – 'Shall I eat your helping?'

No, she would rather just taste it herself, and then the enthusiasm would become general.

His reaction to the completely different surroundings was remarkably adult. The family usually spent the mornings on the beach and the afternoons in the beautiful countryside of the French Riviera. During a picnic in the snow Jan Maarten sat quietly looking about him after grace had been said. The mountains rose white and majestic all round the little valley.

'On mountains and in valleys . . .' he murmured, quoting from a well-known Dutch hymn. 'So God is here too.'

The family drove back home through a countryside in bloom. The weather was fine, the plum trees covered in pale pink blossom, and the children could not stop singing.

'You must stop for half-an-hour, children, you'll all be hoarse.'

So they played 'I spy with my little eye' for half-an-hour and then burst into song again.

Evening fell sooner than Heit expected. The children were drooping. There on the hill before them was a castle Chateau St. Jean, now a hotel. Yes, they could get rooms there, one for Heit and Mem with a room leading off it for Jan Maarten and one for the girls on the other side. It was too good to refuse, and nobody regretted the extra luxury. It was like a fairy-tale. In the impressive dining-hall, where the walls were covered with tapestry, the youngest child sat at table with her hands tucked under her. 'You mustn't do that in a posh hotel,' admonished Mem.

'I can't help it, Mem, I'll crumple up if I don't.' Jan Maarten found it all wonderful . . . the high rooms, the chandelier, the food. After dinner Mem bathed him quickly and put him to bed. Lying in the enormous Louis XV bed, he put his arms around her neck and murmured the beginning of an evening prayer, but before he had recited the first line he was fast asleep.

He won many hearts during the trip through France. There are more mongoloid children in France than in Holland but they are seldom seen. Hardly a day passed without his parents being approached by a stranger.

'Ah, Madame, my eldest son is just like yours,' and then came the question and the sorrow.

'But how, but how is your boy so much more advanced than mine . . .'

No, Jan Maarten is not much better, he is an 'average' mongoloid child. Mother realized that at St. Ursula's. But Jan Maarten's circumstances have resulted in the development of his great capacity to give and to receive love. That is why he is so valued a member of the family.

At the beginning of 1955 there were no omens of the catastrophe that was to befall Jan Maarten that year. He was now an industrious member of the weaving class, and produced dusters, towels and table cloths under the tireless guidance of

Sister Anselma. At home extra attention was paid to reading, writing and arithmetic. His elder sister was now attending a grammar school, the younger was still at primary school. Mem managed to teach a few hours a week again, much to her joy.

In spring Jan Maarten caught 'flu which was followed by a mild infection of the kidneys. He bore the dullness of a saltless diet as bravely as always. The family again stayed at the little *pension* at Juan-les-Pins in April together with Grandmother and a friend of the eldest daughter. It was again a great success. To his sorrow Jan Maarten was not allowed to bathe because of the kidney trouble, but a water bike compensated largely for the deprivation. And of course there were excursions by boat and by car. Jan Maarten joined in everything enthusiastically but tired quickly and liked to keep Grandmother company. He was quite well again in the summer. The lake-side house was always full of cousins and friends in the summer holidays. They came to learn sailing at the nearby sailing school and to pass the summer swimming, rowing and working in the garden. Jan Maarten was also allowed to take a course in sailing with his younger sister and a friend. He found it tiring but thoroughly enjoyed it and really did his best. He slept in the attic in what might be called the 'guest dormitory' with six other boys, who were all very kind and looked after him well. He grew taller and thinner.

68

At the end of August the family spent a week in Brabant. He was tired out from the first day. He dragged himself about, determined to enjoy himself, but it was evident that he was perpetually exhausted. His mother was terribly worried, but she could give no real reason for her anxiety. She took him to the doctor once or twice for minor upsets, but they were not serious in themselves. School was due to start on 3 September, but before embarking on a new school year, his mother took him to their old friend, the family doctor, and repeated what she had said nine years ago:

'I want to see a specialist. There's something wrong and I don't know what.'

Their knowledgeable friend again first checked up before consulting a specialist, and again he discovered what was wrong in a very short time. Jan Maarten had diabetes and had to be admitted to hospital immediately.

He was strangely precocious at this time.

'Do you think I'm going to die?' he asked a close friend of the family.

'But Jan Maarten, what makes you ask that?' she answered with tears in her eyes.

'Because I think I am,' he said calmly.

'Do you think Mary will come and fetch me?' he asked his mother the same evening.

'What would you do if she came?' his mother replied. She sat on the edge of his bed watching his face. She was to take him to hospital next day.

69

'I'd go with her,' said Jan Maarten, happily sure of himself.

'And what about me?' his mother asked involuntarily. She could have bitten out her tongue, but she felt singularly helpless and desolate.

'Yes, it wouldn't be nice for you, but I'd like so much to go,' he said longingly.

This is really the end of the history of what could be called a 'normal' mongoloid child. But fortunately Jan Maarten's history is not yet at an end. It was very difficult for his parents to accept the fact of his diabetes. He himself accepted every setback with such courage and with so little fuss as would put many adults to shame. He drew on reserves of natural cheerfulness and had complete faith and trust in what the adult world had in store for him. He accepted life as God gave it to him.

V

In this last chapter I shall try to emphasize what may be of interest to the parents of older mongoloid children. Of course, Jan Maarten's life has been bound up with the complication of his illness ever since September, 1955. But this in no way affected his potential which was determined by the same factors as that of other mongoloid children.

Jan Maarten spent a month in hospital with his mother. How many 'friends for life' he made there! How great was the help given by the specialist and the matron to the mother as she familiarized herself with the complex of new problems. And how many hearts did Jan Maarten not win as he tried to adapt himself to a new rhythm of life, quietly seeking distraction in weaving and jig-saw puzzles.

At home in October, he gradually returned to normal. His surprise that the doctor was again able to do away with all the unpleasantness was transformed into complete obedience to the new rules. He was able to go back to school in November. St. Ursula's co-operated as always in superhuman fashion. Jan Maarten took his diet with him every morning in a schoolbag, and the Sister whose task it was to prepare a midday dinner for three hundred children found time to cook his meal too. A new watch helped him remind his form-mistress when it was time for his 10-o'-clock snack or his afternoon drink. The regular rhythm of his life gradually established itself and his confidence began to return. But one great drawback manifested itself: his resistance to illness was greatly lowered, and whenever there was an outbreak of an infectious disease at school, Jan Maarten was sure to be the second child to catch it.

In January 1956 a nurse again joined the family to ensure a measure of regularity in Jan Maarten's life in the midst of a busy household. The family's tempo could not be adapted to suit him; Heit's work was demanding and his hours irregular. The number of children in the house varied continually because there was always room in this lakeside haven when family complications occurred in town. Jan Maarten liked people and enjoyed having guests, whom he inevitably welcomed charmingly. But he himself could not be allowed to suffer neglect on their account. It was the none-too-easy task of the nurse to see that this did not happen.

The older boys who stayed in the house for shorter or longer periods were responsible for introducing quite naturally a new phase in the disciplinary side of Jan Maarten's upbringing. His observant eye and sensitivity to moods soon conveyed to him the purport of a 'talk' in Heit's study when Heit wished to 'discuss' certain sins of omission or commission.

'Must I come to your study?' he would ask anxiously when he realized he had done something quite wrong. Heit did not hesitate to seize these opportunities.

'Yes, you come along with me.'

A session in the study has been an effective disciplinary measure ever since.

Before the summer holidays began father and mother decided, in consultation with the Sisters at St. Ursula's, that Jan Maarten would not return to school in September. He was nearly sixteen by this time, and his frequent absences through illness were destroying the beneficial effect of working in the community of the classroom. Jan Maarten had spent nine years at St. Ursula's. In summer he had ridden along the beautiful River Amstel, in winter he had slithered along the winding, slippery polder roads. He had seen many alterations and improvements in the school but one thing remained constant and he benefited from that to the full: the loving, devoted, dedicated hearts of the Sisters of St. Ursula, who endeavour to recognize and stimulate each tiny talent the children assigned to their care may possess. *When conditions at home, whatever they may be, make it impossible to bring up a backward child with his brothers and sisters, he will most certainly be happy in the type of institution Jan Maarten was privileged to attend.* We in Holland are fortunate that so much is done for handicapped children, and done so well.

Yet despite this, there are still a multitude of problems and cares, some of which do not crop up until the child is sixteen. Jan Maarten's father and mother had seldom made long-term plans for the little craft that rode so unsteadily on the waves. But they had departed from this principle, shortly before Jan Maarten was discovered to be diabetic, and they had looked about them to find out what would be best for him after his sixteenth birthday. Arrangements had just been made when he fell ill in August, 1955. He was to have attended an institution for older boys as a day-boy several days a week, for his parents were convinced of the desirability of his sharing duties and activities with boys of his own age. The diabetes changed these plans. It was evident that this frail craft needed a single person at the helm.

'Coming home' was no problem for Jan Maarten. His friend was also leaving school to help his father on the farm; Jan Maarten left school to help the gardener.

Despite a certain amount of variety, we tried to adhere to a fairly regular timetable for Jan Maarten. After breakfast and with the help of the a hike in the mountains, or he would have his snack, at exactly the right time, standing on a platform in a cave by candlelight, watching the stalactite dripping away the time. He was very happy, sharing these experiences with the rest of the family.

The older he became the more he enjoyed our travels. His mother had noticed when he was quite small that he loved beautiful things. Encouraged by this, she had taken him to the Rijks-museum in Amsterdam with his eldest sister. The first visit lasted only half-an-hour and they went back again later. They went to other exhibitions too, but always avoided long visits. These visits were also a source of pleasure, and Jan Maarten soon showed a preference for religious subjects. This interest of his was invaluable when the family went on holiday. He always accompanied them when they went to look at something beautiful and so he could, in his fashion, share their pleasure too.

One year, when the two girls were still at grammar school, the family decided to spend a holiday in Greece with a family of cousins. It was quite a large party that was to set out on this exciting expedition, and plans were discussed on many evenings. Jan Maarten sat quietly listening to the others. He himself looked at pictures of what he would be seeing in Greece with his nurse and he read a simple version of the story of the Trojan

79

War. Once in Greece he happily recognized many of the objects he had 'studied' at home and inevitably raised his hand when the guide mentioned a familiar name. Thus the holiday was as unforgettable for him in his own way as for his sisters. He and Spiros, the chauffeur, who spoke only Greek, wept bitter tears on each other's shoulders when the time came to part. Jan Maarten had often sat next to Spiros, had laughed with him and sung with him. They had thumped each other cheerfully on the back, calling each other 'my friend'. They will not forget each other lightly.

Jan Maarten's ability to listen quietly and absorb what he is capable of understanding stood him in good stead in another important sphere. He liked to accompany the family to church where his father often played the organ. He would sit quietly near him or go up into the gallery. He always listened attentively and joined in the singing during the services. A number of years were devoted to preparing him for confirmation. He read a children's Bible together with a minister and also discussed with him what he had read by himself. When there was family Bible reading at home he frequently recognized the passage as one he had read himself or had discussed with the minister. His prayers were always entirely sincere: he would fervently pray for the safe return of a relation away on a journey or the recovery of a sick friend. His trust in God was and is absolute. He is used to not understanding everything, but he is sure that his trust will not be betrayed. The minister and his parents agree that Jan Maarten can teach them a great deal.

Apart from taking him to church, Heit also occasionally took Jan Maarten shooting or fishing. This happened only rarely, for both activities were rather too strenuous for the boy. But his pleasure in going out with the men was so great that the extra organization it required was well worth while. The experience of joining a shooting party and dining with the sportsmen afterwards gave Jan Maarten a strangely manly air. He then, like some of the other guests, enjoyed making a speech in which there was a compliment or a word of comfort for each.
'Uncle, . . . I still think you're a jolly good shot!'

The diabetes stayed relatively well under control for a number of years. Then dark clouds began to gather over Jan Maarten's head. Father and mother had always kept a careful eye on him ever since the illness had manifested itself. Relations in the medical profession and good friends had often helped to avoid trouble through their interest and advice. But there came a time when they too were powerless. There was something treacherous undermining his strength. His twentieth birthday fell in a period of great weakness. When his friends of the village band came to bring him a morning serenade – which he had hoped against hope they would – he had to lie down every ten minutes because he was too exhausted to stay on his feet.

When Heit and Mem took him to the hospital in January they knew that the seas of life were beginning to swamp the frail craft. It was a miracle that the cause was discovered by an excellent specialist in time and a touch of genius gradually brought about a change in Jan Maarten's apparently hopeless condition.

He recovered very slowly, and this time he emerged from the clouds much more adult than ever before. Every past illness had been forgotten very soon. But he did not forget this one. It was a long time before he regained confidence in his health, but once he had, he was and remained deeply grateful.

A year later speech lessons were started again with the teacher who had first helped him at St. Ursula's. The lesson itself was only an hour a week, but he worked hard at it and soon made progress. Jan Maarten liked to welcome guests at table and his ability to express himself on these occasions improved noticeably.

Even when he was angry he was able to put his thoughts into words now. Mem noticed that one day when, sitting at his bedside, she scolded him

When it was suggested that his speech teacher should give him English lessons, Jan Maarten at first felt honoured, but then said earnestly:

'I'm afraid I'll find it rather hard.'

'That doesn't matter, Jan Maarten; it's good to tackle something difficult.'

He wanted to sleep on it, and the next morning he had decided to take the plunge. After all, he would then be able to talk to our foreign guests. He worked hard at his lessons, learning a few phrases and odd words, helped by the fact that he usually understood most of what was said to him.

'May I bother you for a light?' he asked, daringly, an Australian guest, who promptly started telling him a long story. Nodding and smiling pleasantly as if he understood every word, he tactfully withdrew.

'Just a drop? he asked another, handling the bottle like an experienced bartender.

'Thank you,' said the guest, taking Jan Maarten for granted. Jan Maarten filled his glass carefully, conscious of his responsibility.

The elocution and English lessons helped Jan Maarten's general development and he is still making progress. And now he is twenty-five years old. His 25th birthday was celebrated in grand style. He toasted his guests in wine and declared from the bottom of his heart:

'How glad I am that I'm at last twenty-five.'

There were certainly others who were quite as

glad as he and grateful too. Heit and Mem remembered how he had been given only eight years to live. The decision to enjoy from day to day all the special sweetness this child had brought into their lives traced a golden thread through their memories of twenty-five years.

'What made him like this?' his mother asked herself as she watched him radiant among his guests. 'His heart of gold was a gift he brought into the world when he was born. We have been able to help him acquire the self-discipline which enabled him to overcome his tremendous physical handicaps. The unique place that is his in our small community is a gift from God to us all, for which we can never be grateful enough.'

And Heit put his feelings into the words of the prayer of thanks with which he closed this memorable day:

'Help us to live with our cares and with our blessings.'

VI

The gift of being able to observe quietly and imitate accurately brought Jan Maarten much farther in life than was generally thought possible. In this book I have tried to observe Jan Maarten's progress through life in so far as it might be of interest to other parents. Not that I would wish them to 'imitate'. How utterly impossible it would be to equate one very special case with another. But I have tried to give examples of certain rules which helped us and which helped to create for our son that atmosphere of security in which he was able to develop his limited mental powers and the generous gifts of his heart.

Children like Jan Maarten will in the first place demand of us that we accept them as they are. If we really wish them to share in our family life in a harmonious fashion and still be themselves, they must be accorded a status comparable to that of the other children in every way, including the performance of tasks and the acceptance of discipline. We found our decision to demand of him what we would have of a child of half his age entirely justified and practicable. Of course this is not the only way. But it is important to mark out a clearly defined path that is also acceptable for the other children in the family.

Having chosen a reasonable framework, let us not expect our other children or ourselves to act in a 'special' way. The more 'normal' our behaviour and attitude to the child, the easier it is for the outside world to accept him and relax in his presence. Once a Jan Maarten is given his niche in the family, he will require more vigilance and greater attention than a normal child. We never forgot the warning 'These children are delicate'. They are delicate, they often react differently from other children, but that does not necessarily mean that this fact must be blindly accepted. Jan Maarten was privileged in that the doctor who attended him most frequently was a village doctor who was not easily discouraged.

People are much too apt to generalize about mongoloid children and to say that

they all have a chapped skin,

they all have perpetual colds,

they all have pimples and sores, and

they all have inflamed eyes.

And these are only a few of the remarks to which I object. For their skin is tender, but if their faces are washed with water only once a day and for the rest cleaned with a good cleansing cream, the roughness disappears for good in a short time. Jan Maarten did have a perpetual cold until his tonsils were removed and we left that stage behind. Cuts are inclined to become infected

Eighteen years

Photo: Cas Oorthuys

Twenty-four years

Photo: Cas Oorthuys   Happy in the Hebrides

Twenty-five years   *Photo: Cas Oorthuys*

very soon, and an ointment that draws out the inflammation should always be kept at hand. *If we accustom ourselves to treating every smallest threat with attention, we can prevent many tiresome infections.* The same applies to the eyes. A good eyewash and ointment should always be in the medicine chest. We should learn how to use both properly and use them regularly – throw away every swab immediately after use and always wipe towards the nose. It is no trouble at all to add these medicaments to our first-aid kit. There are so many small, almost professional 'tricks of the trade' a mother should know for any child, but especially for these ones.

Regular medical check-ups are essential too. And it is a good thing to mention to the doctor everything that seems at all strange in the child's behaviour.

The development of a retarded child's restricted mental powers requires our devoted care too. It is wise to read extensively on the subject, but it is certainly not necessary to discover everything oneself. Such children observe carefully and imitate well. Abstract ideas are not their strong point. They find it difficult to grasp ideas like 'more', 'less', 'bigger' and 'formerly'. When they learn something new, they must be helped with great patience to practise it and be praised enthusiastically for every sign of progress. At first every single skill costs tremendous effort,

89

but once they have mastered it, they retain the knowledge and constant practice makes it familiar. They are proud of their achievements.

Their ability to learn new skills, to make progress, continues for a long time. Today more and more is being done with mongoloid children over sixteen, for even then they are still capable of learning. They derive so much pleasure from making something they can give away, that it is really worth while teaching them to weave, make rugs or some other handicraft. They are constructive and enjoy being creatively busy. That is why they can become so useful about the house. They enjoy helping father or mother with such daily chores as they can manage, and they do them carefully and precisely.

The special gift of their warm hearts require the utmost vigilance from those who are privileged to guide their steps along the path of life. I repeat: it is essential to know what you want and to lay down simple, hard and fast rules, for it is thus that these children are given the security they need for their development in every respect. Their ability to distinguish between right and wrong is quite normal and that is a great help. Their natural goodness of heart has free play. They are prepared to do a great deal for others provided they are not spoilt. They respond like flowers in the sun to a word of praise and are quickly upset by disapproval; on the whole they part of his life had now become threats that were ever more difficult to ward off. We who all loved him so, deeply felt our growing helplessness and knew that it could not go on like this.

He himself always wanted to spare our feelings.

'How are you feeling, Jan Maarten?'

'Oh fine, thanks.'

The words were like a sigh in those last weeks.

'You never complain, do you, my boy,' exclaimed his old friend, the specialist. Jan Maarten glanced at him attentively. 'How is your wife?' he asked, interested as always in the well-being of others.

'What shall we read this evening, Jan Maarten?' his father asked on one of the last days.

'Psalm 23, Heit,' and father read 'The Lord is my shepherd, I shall not want.'

When we think of Jan Maarten now, the heart reacts differently from the mind. We remember how when he left school we sought ways of providing activities that he could carry out at home. Afterwards we should have to try to settle his future in some other way, should he survive us. We knew the moment would come when we would have to entrust him to the care of other people. So many parents have to face this problem as their handicapped children grow up. The parting is difficult even when one thinks one has found the best solution, and the vigilant guidance required afterwards is time-consuming and often heartbreaking.

94

EPILOGUE

But now his voyage is over. Life was not easy for Jan Maarten during those two last years. Slowly at first, but none the less surely, the vitality he once had ebbed away. There was a grave crisis, eighteen months before the end, from which he recovered to some extent. A strict diet combined with various medicines managed to keep his health in precarious balance. He continued to busy himself with the activities that remained to him and from which he derived such pleasure: his music, his speech-training lessons, writing birthday letters to his many friends, simple handicrafts, paying visits.

He had one great desire at that time and that was to accompany the family to Scotland where they had already spent several happy holidays. His wish was granted after much thought and preparation. He had many moments of quiet enjoyment with his Scottish friends: half-an-hour's sea-fishing – and he always came home with a respectable catch!–, a short walk to feed the pheasants, a chat using the few words of English he knew. We were all most painfully aware of the unique quality of these days.

The little complications that had always been

Because Jan Maarten fell ill we were spared these problems. For more than twelve years he lived at home, a working, active, irreplaceable member of the family. Irreplaceable – yes, and then the memories come crowding in. All our friends make their contribution to our rich store, for almost each one of them can tell of some specific happening or expression that struck them as being typical of Jan Maarten and which they will always associate with him. Irreplaceable – this word, and all these memories, touch the heart which, knows its own sorrows. How did Jan Maarten always manage to transform our grief and to put us on the track of 'being happy together' in such unexpected ways? With his limited mental capacities and his great heart he had all that is really essential to human happiness. His special way of looking at people and things meant so much to us that our daily life now seems almost colourless without him.

He lived in *our* world in so far as he was able. But the miracle was that he opened up *his* world to us so easily, a world where warmth, humour and sheer happiness reigned and where all activity was directed towards a single goal: how and in what way could he help everyone today?

Jan Maarten was permitted to live among us for far longer than we ever dared hope; and for this we shall always be grateful.